# SINISTER MIX

by

Brian Bowyer

Nocturnal Press Publishing

Also by Brian Bowyer

APOCALYPSE

PERPETUAL DREAD

ROAD HARVEST

SHELF LIFE

GRAVE NEW WORLD

NOCTURNAL BLOOD

GRAVEYARD BLUES

MATTERS OF SHADE

NIGHTHOUSE

DARKER THAN NIGHT

INFINITE DOOM

THE LIGHT OF MEMORY

TIME'S ACCELERATION

DAYLIGHT FADES

WRITING AND RISING FROM ADDICTION

For Carissa

# CONTENTS

## FAMILY PORTRAIT

Melanie sat on the sofa, a glass of beer gone warm on the coffee table, and listened to the clock ticking on the wall.

Bill was at work. Tabitha was at school. And Timothy was six months in his grave.

Melanie closed her eyes, struggling not to cry. If not for their daughter, she doubted her marriage to Bill would survive.

Timothy's death had devastated their family. The cancer had claimed him quickly; he was diagnosed at nine and buried shortly after his tenth birthday. Since then, Bill had been drinking more heavily than ever, Melanie had become addicted to pain medication, and Tabitha—once so happy and vibrant—had withdrawn from almost everything.

Timothy had been one year older than Tabitha, and Tabitha had adored her older brother. Now, when she was home, Tabitha rarely left her room. She almost never spoke, and she barely ate.

Melanie opened her eyes. The clock continued to tick. In twenty minutes she had to pick Tabitha up at school.

Melanie rose and walked into the kitchen, poured away the beer, rinsed and left the glass in the sink. She took a pain pill from a bottle in the cupboard and swallowed it dry, then took a drink from Bill's bottle of whiskey in the freezer. She looked at the clock on the microwave and decided it was time to leave.

Tabitha's school was a ten-minute drive away. Melanie parked near a row of school buses and watched children come tumbling out the door. Most of them laughed and jumped around, but not Tabitha: she simply walked with her head down and got in the car on the passenger's side.

"Would you like to help me make some cookies this afternoon?" Melanie asked.

"No," Tabitha said. "I don't like cookies anymore."

Melanie drove them home. Tabitha went straight to her room. Melanie thought about cooking dinner, then decided instead to order a pizza later. She turned the TV on and fell asleep on the sofa.

***

She woke up less than one hour later. Bill would not be home for another two hours. She went upstairs to check on her daughter, but Tabitha was not in her room. She looked out her daughter's bedroom window and saw Tabitha on her hands and knees in the back yard. She appeared to be digging.

Melanie went downstairs, walked outside, and joined her daughter on the back lawn. Clouds were rolling in from the southwest. Thunder rumbled in the distance. Melanie said, "Are you digging for treasure?"

"No," Tabitha said. "Something else."

Two summers ago, before Timothy was diagnosed with bone cancer, they took a trip to the beach and Bill bought Timothy a plastic shovel. Timothy and Tabitha had used that plastic shovel to dig in the sand on the beach while making a sand castle.

Now, two years later, with her dead brother six months in his grave, Tabitha had evidently found the plastic shovel in Timothy's toy chest and brought it out here to dig around in the back yard. Tears formed in Melanie's eyes. Perhaps Tabitha was pretending that her brother was still alive and they were building an imaginary sand castle.

Lightning fired off on the horizon. Thunder roared. Rain began falling from the darkening sky.

"Come on," Melanie said. "Let's go inside."

Tabitha followed her mother into the house.

***

Bill came home at six and immediately began drinking whiskey. Melanie took a pain pill and ordered a pizza. When it came time to eat, the three of them sat at the kitchen table. They barely ate anything at all.

***

The next day, Saturday morning, Melanie woke up on the sofa. Bill was off work today and Tabitha did not have school. Still groggy from the pain medication in her system, Melanie went upstairs and brushed her teeth in the bathroom. She did not remember falling asleep last night. There were dark circles beneath her bloodshot eyes.

She went into her bedroom. Bill, snoring loudly, was passed out on the bed. The room reeked heavily of alcohol. A nearly-empty bottle of whiskey sat on the nightstand.

She went to Tabitha's room. The door was shut. She opened it and stepped into the room. The unmade bed was empty. She crossed the room and looked out the window.

Rain was falling. The yard was wet. Once again, Tabitha was on her hands and knees, digging. Even from this distance, Melanie could see that her daughter was filthy.

Melanie went back into her bedroom and shook her husband. Bill opened his eyes. “Look outside,” Melanie said.

“What?”

“Our daughter is outside digging in the rain.”

Bill looked over at the bedside clock. “You woke me up to tell me that?”

“She’s digging in the rain. You don’t find that strange?”

Bill reached over, grabbed his whiskey, and finished the bottle. Then he put his head back on the pillow. “It’s my day off,” he said. “You know I like to sleep in. But since I’m awake, why don’t you take your clothes off and join me?” He pulled the blanket aside and clutched his erection.

Melanie said, “You’re disgusting.”

“Why? Because I want to make love to my wife? We haven’t had sex since Timothy died.”

She turned her back on him, went downstairs, and walked outside.

Rain continued to fall. The grass was saturated.

In the back yard, Tabitha was on her hands and knees, still digging. Timothy's plastic shovel lay broken by the hole. Tabitha was now digging with a garden spade that she had taken from the garage. The hole was perhaps a foot wide and a foot deep.

"Come on," Melanie said. "Let's go inside."

Tabitha looked up at her with a distant gaze. She had mud in her hair, on her face, and all over her clothes, arms, and hands. "No, Mommy! I have to dig!"

"You can dig later. Right now, we need to go inside and get you cleaned up."

Melanie leaned over and put a hand on her daughter's shoulder—and Tabitha spun around and smacked her mother in the face with the garden spade. The metal blade struck Melanie's nose and mouth. Her eyes watered and she felt her upper lip split. She put a hand to her face and it came away red with blood.

"I have to dig," Tabitha whispered. She resumed digging in the muddy hole.

"Fine," Tabitha said. "You can dig your way to China for all I care." She went back inside and took a pain pill.

***

Bill came downstairs an hour later. His hair was wet and he wore a bathrobe. He grabbed another bottle of whiskey from the cupboard and cracked it open. “What are we having for dinner?”

Melanie sat at the kitchen table, chopping a pain pill with a razor blade. “I don’t care. Whatever you want.”

Tabitha rushed into the kitchen through the door that opened onto the back yard. She was filthy and tracked mud all over the linoleum floor. “Daddy! I found a skeleton!”

Bill took a shot of whiskey. “A skeleton?”

“Yes! Do you want to see it?”

“Maybe later.”

Tabitha looked at Melanie. “What about you, Mommy? Do you want to see the skeleton?”

“No,” Melanie said. “I’m mad at you for busting my nose and mouth.”

“I’m sorry, Mommy. It was an accident.”

Melanie sliced a soda straw in half with the razor blade. “Okay. I forgive you.”

Tabitha said, “I have to feed the skeleton.” She opened the refrigerator and retrieved a block of half-eaten cheese. “Can I feed it this?”

“Sure,” Bill said. “Whatever the skeleton wants.”

"Thanks, Daddy!" Tabitha dashed outside with the block of cheese.

Bill took another shot of whiskey. "I haven't seen her that excited since her brother died."

Melanie sniffed the crushed pain pill through the soda straw.

***

Later, after Tabitha had finally come in and taken a bath, they had Chinese food delivered from a nearby restaurant. While Bill and Melanie ate, Tabitha talked about the skeleton. "He didn't like the cheese. I'll have to feed him something else tomorrow."

"About this skeleton," Melanie said. "What kind of skeleton is it?"

"I don't know," Tabitha said. "He wouldn't tell me."

Bill said, "How do you know the skeleton was a boy's?"

"Because," Tabitha said. "I just do."

Melanie said, "You need to eat your food."

Tabitha rubbed her eyes. "I'm not hungry. I just want to go to sleep."

***

Melanie woke up on the sofa at four in the morning. As usual, she did not remember going to sleep. She went upstairs and brushed her teeth, then checked on the two remaining members of her family. Bill was passed out drunk, snoring loudly. Tabitha was sound asleep in her bed.

Melanie went downstairs and took a pain pill. She opened the refrigerator and noticed that Tabitha's leftover Chinese food was gone. Had Bill eaten it during an alcoholic blackout? It was certainly possible, although if he had eaten it, there would be evidence of his feeding frenzy all over the floor. Whenever he ate while he was drunk, he usually spilled more food than he consumed.

She looked in the trash can and saw Tabitha's empty Chinese-food container. She smiled, thinking that Tabitha may have woken up hungry during the night and had finally eaten.

Melanie sat down at the kitchen table and lit a cigarette, thinking about her daughter's imaginary talking skeleton in the back yard. She assumed this was Tabitha's way of dealing with the pain of losing her brother, and she hoped it was normal. It was certainly healthier than her own solution to dealing with the pain of losing her son—which was keeping herself so numb on pain medication that she barely felt anything at all.

She finished her cigarette, grabbed a flashlight, and stepped outside.

The night was calm. The sky was starry. The moon resembled a silver, deadly sickle.

She walked to Tabitha's hole and turned on the flashlight. In the hole she saw the rice, beef, and broccoli that she had refrigerated after dinner. Sometime during the night, Tabitha had dumped the food into this hole and then put the empty container in the kitchen trash. Curiously, the block of cheese was gone. Perhaps a wild animal had eaten it, or maybe Tabitha had retrieved it from the hole and put it in the trash.

Melanie went back inside. She searched the trash can. She did not find the half-eaten block of cheese.

She took another pain pill and the world faded away.

***

She woke up at seven a.m. on the sofa. Dust motes floated in the beams of light shining through the windows.

She went upstairs and brushed her teeth. Bill was still passed out. Tabitha was not in her bedroom. Melanie crossed the room and looked out the window.

In the back yard, Tabitha lay flat on her stomach, her head hanging over the edge of the hole. She was not moving.

Melanie rushed downstairs and ran outside. “Tabitha!”

Her daughter did not move.

Melanie fell on the ground beside her and lifted her daughter’s body into her arms. Tabitha’s eyes were closed, but she was breathing.

Then she opened her eyes, and smiled dreamily.

Melanie said, “Are you okay?”

“Hungry,” Tabitha said.

“Of course you are, poor baby. You’ve been out here digging and you haven’t eaten anything.”

“Not me,” Tabitha said. “The skeleton. He ate the cheese and the Chinese food, but he’s still hungry.”

Melanie looked down into the hole. The Chinese food was gone.

She held her daughter close to her body and rocked her on the lawn beside the hole. Tabitha seemed exhausted, but she also seemed content for once to simply be held in her mother’s arms.

“I’m sleepy,” Tabitha said.

Melanie picked her up and carried her inside.

In the living room, Bill sat on the sofa, fresh from bed and already drinking whiskey.

"Little early for that," Melanie said.

"It's Sunday," Bill said. "I always start drinking early on Sundays."

Melanie put Tabitha on the couch beside her father. Then she went back outside to examine Tabitha's hole.

The hole was bigger than it had been yesterday—now perhaps two feet wide and two feet deep. Also, there was another, smaller hole inside the hole. She hadn't noticed it before, and didn't think Tabitha had dug it. She crouched down to look at it more closely.

Slime dripped from the edges of the hole. She thought it resembled a tunnel, or maybe an entrance to a strange creature's burrow. She thought of slithering reptiles, and shuddered. Could a snake have made the hole within the hole? She didn't think so. She thought the tunnel was too large for a snake.

Melanie grabbed the garden spade that Tabitha had been using and began scooping dirt back into the hole. After she finished, she stood and tamped the dirt beneath her feet. The hole was filled. The grass was gone, but the grass would grow again. Satisfied, she went back inside the house.

Bill still sat on the sofa, watching TV.

"Where's Tabitha?" Melanie asked.

"She fell asleep. I took her upstairs and put her in her bed."

Melanie joined her husband on the sofa. She looked at their family portrait on the wall. The portrait had been taken about a year before Timothy was diagnosed with bone cancer. The three surviving people in the portrait looked like strangers; their happiness rendered them unrecognizable. She put her head on her husband's shoulder. "Will we ever be happy again?"

Bill took a shot of whiskey. "I hope so."

"So do I," Melanie said, and then repeated it: "So do I."

***

Tabitha woke up Monday morning with a fever. Melanie gave her some aspirin and kept her home from school. She wanted to take her to a doctor, but Tabitha insisted that—excluding the fever—she otherwise felt fine. "If I'm not better tomorrow, you can take me to the doctor," Tabitha said.

"Okay. What do you want for breakfast?"

"Cheeseburgers."

"Cheeseburgers?"

"Yes. Two of them. One for me, and one for my friend."

Melanie scratched her head. "And who is this friend of yours?"

"The one who was in the hole. I dug him up."

"Tabitha, I filled the hole in yesterday. The hole is no longer there."

"I know that, Mommy. He's not in the hole anymore. He got out. And he's not a skeleton anymore, either. But he still won't tell me his name. He says it's a secret."

Melanie decided to play along. "Fine. Two cheeseburgers, coming right up."

They went downstairs. Tabitha followed her mother into the kitchen. She sat at the table while Melanie fried beef patties on the stove.

Soon thereafter, Melanie placed two plates on the table. On each plate was a cheeseburger with potato chips. "Better call your friend," Melanie said, "before the food gets cold."

"Put them in my room," Tabitha said. "I'm not hungry anymore."

"Honey, you need to eat."

"We'll eat them later!"

"Calm down," Melanie said. Then she took the food upstairs to Tabitha's room.

She noticed right away that the bedroom window was open. The parted curtains billowed softly in a breeze. Had the window been open previously? She didn't remember opening it, nor did she think that Tabitha was strong enough to lift it by herself. Perhaps Bill had opened it before he went to work. The pain medication was ruining her short-term memory. She put the two plates of food on Tabitha's bed and closed the window.

She went in the bathroom and brushed her teeth. Then she went back downstairs.

Tabitha was in the living room, watching cartoons. Melanie took a pain pill and joined her on the sofa.

***

She woke at noon. The television was still on, but Tabitha wasn't with her on the sofa. Melanie rose, stretched, and turned the TV off. Then she went upstairs to check on Tabitha.

Her daughter's door was closed. Melanie opened it.

Tabitha lay on her bed completely naked, and she wasn't alone. There was something snuggled up against her, nestled close to her in the crook of her arm. It was gray, pink, and covered in slime, a writhing lump about the size of a fire extinguisher. Its mouth was attached to Tabitha's neck.

Horror froze Melanie momentarily, but then fear for her daughter propelled her forward. She approached the bed. The thing turned and looked at her. It had two bright blue eyes and a mouth full of vicious-looking teeth. She grabbed the thing and pulled it off her daughter.

Surprisingly, it wasn't as cold and slimy as it looked. In fact, it was warm and exquisitely soft. It smelled like Tabitha. It smelled like Timothy and Tabitha had smelled when they'd been babies. That was exactly what it smelled like: a harmless, helpless little baby. She had not realized how much she had missed that delicious, intoxicating scent.

She pressed her face against the creature and inhaled. "My baby," she said. "I want to be the only one who feeds you."

It nuzzled its head against her breasts in response. She removed her blouse and put a nipple in its mouth. The creature began to feed.

Bleeding, Melanie sat down on the bed with her baby. Tabitha's eyes were open, but she was dead. Needlessly, Melanie checked for a pulse that wasn't there. Then she gently closed her daughter's eyes.

***

Bill got home at six. The house was quiet. He went in the kitchen and grabbed a bottle of whiskey. He took a few drinks and felt better immediately.

While crossing the living room, he stopped and stared at the portrait of his family. Before the bone cancer, the four of them had been so happy together.

*Oh well,* he thought. *At least the three of us still have each other.*

He took another drink, and nodded. "Things could be worse," he told the portrait.

Then he turned and headed up the stairs.

## FIRST DATE

"Do you always drink this much?" Holly asked Mark with no accusation in her voice. She looked like she might be curious but she didn't strike him as the judgmental type.

He took another drink from his third glass of bourbon. "Yes. I'm an alcoholic."

Holly stirred her own drink—a cocktail the color of a sunrise—with a swizzle stick. "Your honesty is refreshing. Plus, you're a writer. A lot of great writers are alcoholics."

They sat in a booth. The restaurant had a bar in it.

"So," Holly said, "do you do this often?"

"Do I do what often?"

"Go out on dates with women who are fans of your fiction."

Mark shook his head. "No. Not often."

"Do you go out on many dates?"

He shrugged. "I got divorced a year ago. I've been dating on and off since then. Mostly off. But you're definitely the prettiest girl I've been out with."

She rolled her eyes and sat back—but not before she smiled. He could see that she appreciated the compliment. He could also see that she didn't mind being referred to as a girl.

Like him, Holly was in her mid-30s, but looked ten years younger. She had long, wavy auburn hair and bright green eyes. She wore no makeup and didn't need it: her fresh face was beautiful.

And Mark—despite over twenty years of hard drinking—still got carded for cigarettes. He was tall, thin, and (excluding a shorter hairstyle) didn't look much different than he had looked as a teenager.

"What about you?" Mark said. "Do you date often?"

Holly shook her head. "No, not often. I've been a widow for two years now, but I have a lot of children. It's hard to date when you have a lot of children."

He wondered how many children she had. Three or four, maybe? He resisted an urge to ask her. Instead he sipped his bourbon. “I have a daughter named Amber,” he said. “She’s eleven.”

Holly sipped her cocktail. “She’ll be old enough to go out on her own dates soon.”

Mark finished his bourbon. “If she’s not already. I lost my virginity at age eleven.”

“You’ve got me beat,” Holly said. “I was fourteen.”

Mark summoned a waiter, ordered another round, and soon thereafter the man brought him a fourth glass of bourbon.

Holly sat forward again and crossed her arms on the table. “The last guy I went out with didn’t look anything like his profile picture, which for me was a sort of dreaded expectation.”

“Oh yeah?”

“Yes. He was older, had less hair, and was much heavier than he appeared in his picture. I was so pleased to see that you look even better in person than you do in your author photos.”

Mark smiled. “Thanks. You look even better in person, too.”

“So tell me,” Holly said, “about the worst date you’ve been on so far.”

"I met a woman for drinks not long ago and everything was going great—until we ended up back at her place and her parents were inside waiting for us."

"Seriously?"

"Yes. Turned out, the mother was a fan of my work. The father told me that he didn't like to read books, but that his wife had read all of my books and that she wanted me to sign her copy of my vampire novel. The mother wouldn't speak to me at all."

"That's weird."

"Yes. She just kept staring at me and smiling at me the whole time. Anyway, I signed her book, and then the father thanked me and apologized for bothering us. As they were leaving, he whispered into my ear that if I hurt his daughter, he would be forced to kill me."

"Are you kidding me?"

"No."

"So then what happened?"

"I pretended I was sick and called a cab. After that, though, the woman stalked me for about a month. I blocked her as much as I could, of course, but then her father called and left me a voicemail. He apologized for threatening me, said that he had only been joking in the first place, and then told me that if I didn't give his daughter a second chance, he would make me regret it."

"Did you go to the police?"

"No." Mark took a drink. "I got a new phone."

Holly laughed. Then she sipped her cocktail. "Well, you don't have to worry about *my* parents. My father's dead, and the only book my mother ever reads is the bible."

***

They ended up at Mark's apartment.

"Damn," Holly said. "This place is spotless."

Mark shrugged. "I have no pets and I live alone. Keeping it clean is easy."

"I've never lived alone," Holly said. "Do you have any beer?"

He got her a beer and poured himself a glass of bourbon.

***

Later, lying naked beside Mark on his bed, Holly said, "That was amazing."

Mark lit a cigarette. "Yes. It certainly was."

"You've probably been with a lot of women, haven't you?"

He shrugged.

She sat up on the bed and sipped her beer. "How many?"

"I honestly don't know. I've been with a lot of women in blackout, so there's no way I can give you an accurate number."

"A hundred? Two hundred?"

He shrugged again. "Yeah, probably something like that. But I *can* tell you that without alcohol the number would be a whole lot less."

"I've been with two men now," Holly said. "The father of my children, and you."

Mark wasn't sure if he believed her. In any event, he didn't know what to say to that, so he didn't say anything.

Holly sipped her beer. "Would you have had sex with me if you weren't drinking?"

Mark sipped his bourbon. "No offense, but if I weren't drinking, I probably would have never agreed to meet you. Without alcohol, I don't even know how to talk to women. Or anyone else, for that matter. It's one of the reasons I've been drinking for all these years, even though booze has pretty much ruined every relationship I've ever had."

Holly finished her beer. Then she stretched back out and put her head on Mark's chest. "Are you glad you agreed to meet me, or do you regret it?"

"I'm glad. I'm very glad, in fact. I'm hoping this is the beginning of something beautiful."

"Me too," Holly said. Soon, she was asleep.

***

Mark was awake when Holly woke up around eight o'clock in the morning. He had already showered and shaved, and sat working on his current novel in the living room while drinking his first bourbon of the day.

She entered the living room in last night's clothes and joined him on the sofa.

He put his laptop on the coffee table. "Good morning. Did you sleep well?"

"I did. I also found your spare toothbrushes beneath the sink and opened one. Hope you don't mind."

He smiled. "Of course not. That's what they're for. Would you like some breakfast? I have plenty of cereal and skim milk."

"No thanks. But I would love a cup of coffee."

"All I have is instant."

"I love instant coffee."

"How do you take it?"

"Lots of cream and lots of sugar."

She followed him into the kitchen and he made her a cup of coffee. The window above the sink provided a sunlit view of downtown from seventeen stories up.

"I suppose I need to get back to the farm soon," Holly said.

"The farm?"

"Yes. I live on a farm."

Mark finished his bourbon. "You're joking, right?"

"No. I live on a farm."

"I didn't know there were any farms in the city."

Holly smiled. "I don't think there are. I live about an hour away, upstate."

Mark poured more bourbon into his glass. "Sorry. I'm having a hard time wrapping my mind around this. Why on earth do you live on a farm?"

"The farm belonged to my husband's parents. They died before I met him. He owned the farm when I married him, but he died a couple of years ago. Then, after my father passed away, I let my mother come and live with my children and me."

Mark sipped his bourbon. "So now it's you and your mom and your kids all living on the farm."

"Yes. It's a nice farm. You should come and spend the day with me."

He took another drink. "I don't know. I need to work on my book today."

"So bring your laptop. You can work on your book there. The house is very large. I also have a guesthouse. A change of scenery might be good for your writing."

Mark smiled. "That actually sounds kind of fun. Do you have Wi-Fi?"

"Of course I have Wi-Fi. I live on a farm, not in a cave. You can ride up with me, if you want. I can drive you back tonight or in the morning."

"Okay." Other than toiletries, all he packed were two bottles of bourbon and his laptop.

***

The farm was large and isolated. Various types of fencing surrounded the property. Mark saw scattered horses, cows, and tractors across the fields, the majority of which were bordered by hedgerow and woodlot. Holly parked in front of the farmhouse, which was massive. The guesthouse beside it was bigger than Mark's apartment. He saw a large barn nearby and a few smaller barns in the distance.

They got out of the car and went inside the farmhouse. As she led him around the house, he counted six children spread out on the first floor, and he heard what sounded like many more thumping around upstairs. All of the kids he saw looked similar—black hair, pale sexless faces, plain clothes—and none of them looked anything like their mother. They also looked like they had not been out in the sunlight much at all.

"Can I get you anything?" Holly said.

"No thanks. I just want to sit down somewhere and work on my book."

She led him into a spare bedroom with an adjoining bathroom. "Is this okay?"

He took a drink of bourbon. "This is perfect."

She smiled. "Okay. You know where the kitchen is. Just make yourself at home. I'll be around here somewhere. If you need me, just call or send me a text."

She left and closed the door.

Mark took another drink and sat down with his laptop.

***

Time had a way of contracting when Mark was writing. It also seemed to do that when he was drinking.

Whenever he wrote and drank at the same time, time seemed to not exist at all.

He checked his phone. The time was 3:09 p.m. They had arrived at the farm around ten o'clock in the morning. He had been writing for almost five hours and his fifth of bourbon was over halfway empty. Fortunately, the other bottle he had brought with him was even bigger. The half-gallon would last until tomorrow if he decided to spend the night.

Realizing he was hungry, he stepped out of the spare bedroom.

The long hallway was empty, but he heard a lot of kids making noise throughout the house. He also heard more kids running and thumping around upstairs. *Sounds like a daycare,* he thought. But the noise hadn't bothered him while he'd been writing. Mark was never easily distracted whenever he was writing. Plus he was drunk, and very little bothered him at all when he was drunk.

He went into the kitchen and made a couple of sandwiches. He took them back to his room and ate them. He smoked a cigarette and brushed his teeth. Then he took a few more drinks and passed out for a while.

***

Mark woke up two hours later and wrote for about an hour. The writing was going well, and he was pleased with his progress.

Holly entered the room around seven o'clock. She had changed clothes. Her long auburn hair was unbound. "Dinner's ready, if you're hungry."

"I'm hungry for you. You look ravishing. Do we have time for a quickie?"

She smiled and closed the door. "Of course."

They made love. The sex was fast but satisfying for them both.

Then Mark filled his bourbon glass and followed Holly into the dining room.

Holly introduced him to her mother, who sat at one end of the long dinner table. She was old, but still pretty. She looked a lot like Holly, but her hair was gray.

"Nice to meet you," Mark said.

"Likewise."

Seated around the table were ten children of indeterminate sex and age. They all looked so similar with their shaggy black hair and pale flesh that Mark couldn't tell which ones were boys, which ones were girls, or how old any of them were. And none of them looked anything like Holly.

Bewildered, Mark simply smiled and nodded. Then he took a drink of bourbon and sat down.

No one spoke during dinner, so Mark ate in silence like everyone else. In addition to the ten children at the dinner table, he still heard at least that many (if not more) running and thumping around upstairs. Was it possible that Holly was the mother of twenty or more children? She had told him that she was thirty-five, and that she had lost her virginity at fourteen, so maybe she delivered her first baby at fifteen and then kept popping one out every year for the next twenty years. And maybe there were some twins or triplets or quadruplets in the mix. All the kids looked so much alike it was uncanny. If not for the bourbon, he undoubtedly would have found the children unnerving.

*Maybe I'll write a story about it sometime,* he thought. *What I won't do is ask Holly one single question about this lunacy. If she wants to tell me her story, she can tell me on her own. If not, I'll use my imagination.* He took a drink of bourbon, and smiled.

"Is something funny?" Holly's mother said.

"No." He took another drink. "I was just thinking about how nice it is to be out of the city for a while."

After dinner, the children—as one—gathered the dishes and put everything away.

Holly's mother got up and left the room without a word.

"Want some dessert?" Holly said.

Mark finished his bourbon. "No thanks. I believe I'll smoke a cigarette and take another nap."

"Very well. Have you decided if you're going home or staying here tonight?"

"I think I'll stay here. The writing's going well. I'm sure I won't sleep long, and then I'll probably want to stay up and write all night."

Holly smiled. "Excellent. I'll be in my room. If you go up the stairs at the end of the hallway, my bedroom's the last door on the left."

***

Mark did not sleep long. He woke up and took a drink of bourbon. Then he brushed his teeth and took another drink. He checked his phone to see what time it was (10:06 p.m.) and saw a message from Holly: *Hi Mark. A vicious migraine hit me after dinner. The pain's so bad I'm nauseous. I took an OxyContin, so I'll probably sleep the whole night through. Happy writing! See you in the morning.*

He wrote for what seemed like no time at all, but when he checked his phone (1:22 a.m.) he saw that he had been writing for over three hours. He also saw that his phone was almost dead and thought: *I forgot to bring a charger.*

He finished his bourbon and poured another glass. Then he searched the room for a charger, but didn't find one. He decided to walk around the house for a bit. Maybe he would get lucky and find a charger lying around. Taking his bourbon with him, he opened the door and stepped out into the long, empty hallway.

The house was silent at this hour. As he headed toward the living room, the only sounds he heard were his own footsteps on the hardwood floor.

He didn't find a charger in the living room, or in the kitchen, but he did find Holly's mother in the dining room. She was seated at the dinner table, reading a bible by candlelight.

She heard him and looked up. "Come here, Mark. I want to talk to you."

He approached her and took a drink of bourbon. Then he sat down on a chair across from her and took another drink. On closer inspection he saw that she had not been reading a bible, but had instead been reading one of his novels—his vampire novel, specifically.

"You shouldn't be out of your room," she said. "You're not safe here."

"Not safe?"

"No. The children don't want you here. I know you rode up with Holly, and that she's in bed with a migraine, but I can drive you back to the city right now if you will let me. It's your only chance."

"My only chance?"

"Yes. Your only chance to survive. Otherwise, you will die."

Mark took a drink of bourbon. "No thanks. I think I'll just wait and talk to Holly in the morning."

"Very well. Don't say I didn't warn you."

He heard something behind him. There was a sudden blur of movement and then one of the children stuck a knife into his left eye and ruined it. He stood up, but the pain was so intense it dropped him to his knees. He drew in a deep breath to scream and felt a rag being shoved into his mouth. Then he felt a thick band of tape being wrapped around his lips and the back of his head.

With the same efficiency they had displayed earlier while clearing the dinner table, the children tied him up and dragged him outside into the largest of the nearby barns.

Fluorescent lights high up on the ceiling provided bright illumination.

With his remaining eye, he saw more children inside the barn—thirty at least. All had the same black hair and pale, sexless faces.

He also saw several half-eaten cadavers of men hanging by ropes from the rafters. The ropes had been tied around the wrists of the cadavers, so they hung with their arms above their heads and most of their legs eaten away. One of the cadavers had been eaten away all the way up to its chest.

A few of the children tied one of the ropes dangling from the rafters around Mark's wrists. When they finished, he was hanging with his arms above his head and his feet about a foot off the floor.

And then a child led into the barn—on a leash—the biggest pig Mark had ever seen. The pig had to weigh a thousand pounds at least. Its leash was connected to a thick chain around its massive neck. Despite its size, the pig allowed itself to be led by the small child like a puppy.

As one, every child inside the barn began chanting three syllables in unison: dom-vee-lay. Mark didn't know if it was one word or three words or maybe even the pig's name but those were clearly the three syllables they were pronouncing.

"DOM-VEE-LAY! DOM-VEE-LAY! DOM-VEE-LAY!"

Mark didn't know a lot about the children but he understood this much: their god was a pig; this barn was their cathedral; and tonight, he would be their sacrifice.

"DOM-VEE-LAY! DOM-VEE-LAY! DOM-VEE-LAY!"

A few children walked up to Mark with knives and cut his clothes away, stripping him naked. Two of them cut his legs open—not very deep, but enough to make him bleed.

"DOM-VEE-LAY! DOM-VEE-LAY! DOM-VEE-LAY!"

The child holding the leash led the pig right up to Mark's feet. The giant pig sniffed Mark's blood, and then licked him.

"DOM-VEE-LAY! DOM-VEE-LAY! DOM-VEE-LAY!"

With the pig's first bite, Mark screamed.

He knew his last night on Earth would be the longest of his life.

## MATERNAL FLAME

Nicholas—and that was his name; he didn't like anyone calling him Nick—was only six years old, but he already knew what he wanted to be when he grew up: he would become a paleontologist and dig up dinosaur bones. Those massive, prehistoric creatures fascinated him. His favorite cartoons were those of *The Land before Time* series, and he had watched *Jurassic Park 1*, *2,* and *3* so many times that he had every line of dialogue and action sequence memorized. His favorite TV personality—by far—was Steve Irwin, the Crocodile Hunter, and the only animals that really interested him were reptiles. Dogs were okay, friendly and loyal and everything, but he wasn't allowed to have one of those in his mother's apartment anyway. He kept a pet iguana named Mercer in his bedroom. Mercer was bright green and *huge*—at least two feet long counting his tail. Mercer lived in a big cage, usually remained motionless, and always moved his eyeballs around. He was named after Ron Mercer of the Chicago Bulls, before he had been traded to the Indiana Pacers. Mercer's tongue was even longer than his claws, and Nicholas often wondered if perhaps, millions of years from now, lizards would once again grow to their original gargantuan sizes.

It was Saturday, so he was in his bedroom instead of his first-grade classroom. His TV was set to Cartoon Network; Tom chased Jerry across the screen. He didn't much care for cats and mice, and he therefore inserted *The Land before Time 3* into his ancient DVD player.

His mother, Helen, was a waitress and by no means wealthy, but made sure he never ran out of movies to watch or toys to play with.

His father, Gaston, was a musician searching for stardom out in Los Angeles. Gaston sent woeful letters that rarely contained child-support payments, and if he didn't make it as a rock star, Nicholas figured that he would take care of his father in the future, when he was a successful paleontologist excavating T-Rex skeletons from Dinosaur Quarry in Utah and Colorado.

Helen knocked on her son's bedroom door.

Nicholas, sketching at his art table, swiveled in his chair. “Come in.”

His mother opened the door and entered his room. At twenty-two, as she stood there in her robe, she was easily the prettiest lady he had ever seen.

“Hi, Mom.”

“Good morning. What are you drawing?”

“Just some dragons and some vultures and some lava.”

Helen approached the sketchbook on his table for closer inspection. She thought the drawing was good, and told him so.

“Thanks.”

“You’re welcome. And it’s Saturday, thank God. What would you like to do today?”

Nicholas put his pencil down and stood up. “I don’t know. Anything.”

“Want to go to the mall and look around? Maybe catch a movie?”

“Sounds good to me.”

They enjoyed a breakfast of cold cereal, toast, and chocolate milk, then took turns brushing their teeth, showering, and getting dressed before heading to the mall.

***

When Helen—who had only been checking the prices of video games for a few seconds—turned around in the department store and discovered that her son wasn't right beside her, she didn't immediately panic. He had probably gone off on his own looking at toys. But when she didn't see him in the next aisle over, or the next one or the next, nor, indeed, anywhere in the toy section, a dread the likes of which she had never experienced seized her fully. He would not have wandered out of the toy section. No other items in the store would have interested him whatsoever. The word *abduction* came to mind, but she told herself to not even entertain that theory, that if she refused to consider that horrible possibility, it wouldn't be true. No one could have stolen Nicholas from her, could they? No. That was absurd. Sure, it was becoming a sort of national epidemic in the media, with new children being kidnapped seemingly every day.

But not *her* child, surely.

Dear God, *please*, not her precious Nicholas.

She went in search of her son, running around the store, yelling his name.

She found him nowhere.

One of the managers got his description and began paging through the intercom for Nicholas or anyone who may have seen him to please come to the service desk.

Helen and some of the store's employees and a few customers looked throughout the building. They checked the restrooms, dressing rooms, all departments, beneath counters, the concession area up front amidst the video games and vending machines, even the layaway bins in back, which were filling quickly with Christmas only a couple of months away.

And then Helen was paged to report to the service desk.

*Please, God*, she thought, *let him be standing there, smiling, wondering what all the fuss was about.*

But he wasn't there.

There was only a manager and two young employees in uniform, a teenage boy and girl. They weren't smiling.

Helen said, "What is it? Why did you page me?"

The manager said, "These associates work in the warehouse, and they saw a boy that fits your child's description leave the building with a man through the shipping-and-receiving doors."

"A man?" Helen said. "What kind of man? What did he look like?"

"A white man," the girl said. "About fifty, maybe. Average height and weight, with black hair turning gray."

Helen said, "It may not have been Nicholas. What was the little boy wearing?"

The male associate said, "Blue jeans and a Bulls jersey. Pippen's old number, thirty-three."

That matched his outfit. But had he been wearing number thirty-three or twenty-three? Helen couldn't remember.

She rushed to the back of the store, then outside through the shipping-and-receiving doors.

What she found right off the bat seemed to crack her heart in half. It was Nicholas's little pea-green cloth lizard stuffed with beads that she'd bought him two years ago at the carnival when he'd been four. He loved it so much that he carried it with him everywhere he went. She bent over, picked it up, held it to her face, and smelled it. The tears came then, and with them she lost the strength to stand. She sat down on the asphalt, closed her eyes, and prayed while crying quietly.

A man's voice interrupted her supplication.

She opened her eyes and looked up.

A police officer and the manager were standing beside her.

The policeman said, “Do you have a cellphone?”

“No,” Helen said. “I can’t afford one.”

“Do you have a phone at home?”

“Yes.”

“Then we need you to go home, right away, in case he escapes and makes it to a telephone.”

“Yes,” Helen said, grasping on to any hope remaining. “He may break free and try to call me.”

She had never driven as fast in her life as she drove back to her apartment.

She paced the floors, and wept hysterically, and drank cups of coffee one after another to ensure she would stay awake, even though she knew that sleeping would be impossible.

Darkness claimed the city around eight-thirty, and her phone rang at nine minutes after nine. Helen lifted the receiver on the first ring. “Nicholas?”

“No. It’s me.” *Barb, her best friend at the diner.* “Helen, I’m so sorry. I saw the story on the news—”

“I can’t talk right now,” Helen said. “In case he calls.”

She hung the phone up, turned the TV on, and tuned to CNN. She read the headline *Six-year-old Nicholas Twain Abducted from Mall in Chicago* on the leftward-moving ticker at the bottom of the screen.

She walked into the kitchen. Her hands shook so badly that she had trouble splashing a shot of bourbon into her coffee.

When she returned to the living room, the network was airing the full story. A picture of Nicholas (the one she had given the policeman before speeding home) was on the screen. The sight of him smiling, on television, under these circumstances, made her cry so hard she started hyperventilating.

The phone rang. She caught her breath immediately in a fit of maternal instinct, lifted the receiver, and again said, “Nicholas?”

It wasn’t Nicholas. It was Carrie, another of her waitress friends. Helen quickly explained that she couldn’t talk, and hung up the phone.

This went on until nearly midnight, as more and more people called as soon as they heard the news. Nicholas’s teacher; her boss and more friends from the diner; mothers of her son’s first-grade classmates; Gaston, in Los Angeles, saying he'd be on the next flight to Chicago.

But Nicholas never called.

Helen prayed to God over and over for merciful deliverance of her son back into her loving arms, safe and unharmed and alive.

An artist's composite sketch of the kidnapper—based on the descriptions provided by the two witnesses—was displayed on the TV screen, and Helen screamed at the drawing and begged it to release Nicholas as if the picture could somehow hear her.

She was still crying and sipping whiskey-spiked coffee when dawn transformed the longest night of her life into morning.

Her phone finally rang at five past noon. It wasn't Nicholas. It was someone informing her that a young boy's corpse had been discovered by a maid in a motel room. Could she come down to the morgue and give an ID—positive or negative—on the body?

She told the man that she was in no condition to drive, and he in turn informed her that a ride would be arriving for her shortly.

Before he hung up, Helen said, "Wait. You've seen the body, right?"

"Yes."

"And you've seen the picture of my son?"

"Yes."

"Well then just tell me. Is it Nicholas or isn't it?"

"Well, ma'am, to be perfectly honest … we can't tell one way or the other."

A patrolman, soon thereafter, knocked on her apartment door, and while en route to the morgue, he said only, "I'm sorry about your loss. I'm a father myself. I sure hope this turns out not to be your son."

At the morgue, the officer and an attendant led Helen to where the child's corpse was stored.

When the steel slab was pulled out of its cold holding cell, Helen was revolted by the body's condition, but relieved to see that this couldn't possibly be her Nicholas. She was a good, moral woman and mother. And Nicholas was such a bright and loving child that God was far, far too merciful (wasn't He?) to allow her son to be so thoroughly tortured and defiled.

This corpse was faceless. The skin had literally been torn away. There was only muscle and gristle that was shockingly red over the whiteness of bone. There were two gaping holes where the nose should've been, and the eyes, ears, and lips, too, had been removed. The empty eye sockets seemed abnormally large. Only broken pieces of teeth remained in the mouth, and the tongue was gone. The top of the head had been scalped to the skull.

And then, on closer inspection, she saw that the head wasn't connected to the neck. It had simply been positioned where it had been prior to decapitation.

The horrors got worse.

The arms were placed together from hands to wrists to elbows to shoulders; the fingers from tips to middle joints to knuckles. Ten toes had been placed in correct order at the ends of both feet, which had been hacked off at the ankles. The legs were severed at shins, knees, and thighs. There were stitches up the abdomen, as if the child had been eviscerated and then—later—sewn up by a professional. A couple of body parts were still missing.

It was a once-living jigsaw puzzle of human flesh and bone, covered in ragged black holes that could only be cigarette burns.

Helen vomited a liquid mixture of coffee, bourbon, and bile all over the floor. "I'm sorry," she said. "That's just … I mean … the cruelest thing … I've ever seen."

"Nonsense," the officer said. "I puked myself an hour ago. And I hate it that you have to see this. But the team here did the best they could, and we still couldn't ID this poor, poor little boy."

"That's not Nicholas," Helen said.

"Are you positive?"

"Yes. That's not my son. It can't be."

"So there's nothing here whatsoever that you recognize?"

She pulled her hair out of her face. "No." And then, almost as an afterthought, she added, "I know it isn't him. But, just to be sure . . . roll over the left lower leg."

The attendant, with gloved hands, clutched the section between ankle and knee. "This part?"

"Yes."

He did, and when Helen saw the light brown birthmark shaped faintly like a crescent moon on Nicholas's left calf, she passed out.

***

She came to in a hospital room. Consciousness brought with it no reprieve from this nightmare. Her son was gone, and he had suffered unspeakable atrocities before his crossing.

Helen thought little of a god that would allow it.

She emerged from the raised bed, got dressed, and took the elevator down to the first floor, not bothering to check herself out of the hospital.

Helen wasn't wearing a wristwatch, but the autumn sun's position indicated that the time of day was early evening. The sky was royal blue and cloudless. The wind blowing off Lake Michigan whipped her auburn hair in every direction.

She couldn't abandon Nicholas's lizard to starvation.

She approached the street and hailed a cab to her apartment. She paid her fare, tipped the driver, and then headed straight for Nicholas's bedroom.

Mercer was perched on a branch in his cage, motionless but for those roving eyeballs.

She retrieved the iguana by his underbelly. She barely felt the pricks when his claws scratched her forearms and wrists.

Outside, she released Mercer in the grass at the parking lot's perimeter, and the iguana stalked toward the certain death that waited in downtown Chicago.

Helen walked west, toward the sun, to the nearest filling station down the street. Two pumps in front were available, but she didn't want anyone trying to save her.

She walked behind the store. The diesel pumps, thankfully, were deserted.

"Nicholas, I'm on my way, baby. Wait for me, okay? Mommy's coming. I'll see you soon."

She prepaid with her card and pressed the button that activated the pump. She grabbed a nozzle, aimed it at her face like a pistol, and began hosing herself thoroughly with diesel fuel. She soaked her hair and face with her eyes closed, then opened her eyes and drenched her blouse, her arms and hands, her jeans, her sneakers, and even the pavement around her in a petroleum rain.

Helen retrieved a lighter from her pocket and ignited herself. Flames engulfed her immediately. She curled up like a fetus on the asphalt and screamed. Her last coherent thought before darkness claimed her was that fire, indeed, is the purest form of cleansing.

## YERSINIA-Z

In the passenger's seat of their stolen motorhome, Sally coughed. She retrieved a tissue from the glove box and blew her nose, then wadded the tissue up and tossed it out the window.

Steve, behind the steering wheel, took a drink of whiskey. "Yersinia-Z?" He handed her the bottle.

She took a drink. "No. My bronchitis is acting up." She screwed the cap back on the bottle and placed it between her feet.

"Good," Steve said. "I don't know what I'd do if I lost you."

Sally lit a cigarette. "Same."

Yersinia-Z struck the planet six weeks ago, and it was far more destructive than the Black Death that killed millions of Europeans in the middle ages. A new breed of pneumonic plague that swiftly claimed the lives of billions worldwide, no one knew what caused Yersinia-Z. It spread too quickly for anyone to pinpoint its origin. It was a global catastrophe, wiping out the majority of citizens on all continents equally.

At the plague's onset, before the TV screens went blank, most newscasters denied reports of chemical and biological terrorism, and some—if Sally remembered correctly—indicated that Yersinia-Z began somewhere overseas. They had spoken of AIDS victims raping babies to cure their illness in a village where people worshiped gorillas. On conservative radio stations, religious pundits had preached about how the pestilence had been prophesized two thousand years previously.

Ever since Yersinia-Z struck the planet six weeks ago, Sally and Steve—both nineteen—had been living like kings among the deceased. The dead of Greater Los Angeles were everywhere: in the streets and drainage ditches, decomposing; rotting in clusters of thousands in shopping malls; wasting away atop the palisades in ultramodern mansions.

They pillaged the city relentlessly, filling their motorhome with firearms and ammunition looted from abandoned pawn shops, alcohol lifted from empty liquor stores, and a fortune in currency swiped from cash registers, ATMs, and the purses, wallets, and pockets of corpses crowding the metropolis.

The new rule was lawlessness: all men, women, and children for themselves—but chaos rarely ensued. There were too few people left alive in Los Angeles for competitive warfare to bloom.

Curious was the fact that most survivors—like themselves—happened to be chronic alcoholics.

Sally grabbed the bottle and took a drink. "Where are we going?" She handed the bottle to Steve.

"To the beach at Santa Monica." He took a drink and gave the bottle back.

"Do you promise to kill me? If I get Yersinia-Z?"

"Yes." He stared straight ahead at the road. "But I believe we're immune to the disease. I believe we'll be fine as long as we keep drinking this whiskey."

***

Justin had always known that nature—like himself—was a serial killer, for all things born are only born to die. But now that nature had lost its patience and unleashed this plague upon the planet, there were precious few creatures left to slaughter.

Yersinia-Z didn't exterminate humans exclusively. The number of feline and canine carcasses in the streets was staggering, and the dead birds outnumbered the multitude of human corpses decomposing in Los Angeles enormously. Justin had never realized how many birds existed until they started dying and dropping from the sky. He now barely noticed when their skeletons crunched beneath his feet.

Even the rats were succumbing to Yersinia-Z, emerging from the sewers with red whiskers to asphyxiate on the misplaced blood oozing from their snouts.

Justin did, however, encounter humans occasionally, and all of them were (like him) chronic alcoholics. He murdered these people—these survivors of the new pneumonic plague—and consumed them, because he didn't wish to eat infected meat.

Sometimes he cooked the flesh, and sometimes he didn't. But he always chased his meals with a fifth of whiskey.

***

Steve parked the motorhome behind Santa Monica Visitor Center. The streetlamps still glowed six weeks after the end of civilization. Though the chance was slim that anyone would steal their belongings, Steve locked the doors and engaged the alarm system after he and Sally exited the motorhome.

Human and animal corpses lay scattered all over the parking lot, but with the sun's absence, and the night wind, and the salty scent of the sea, the stench of decay wasn't as bad as it was during the day.

Sally took a drink of whiskey and gave the bottle to Steve, then lit a cigarette and looked up at the starry sky. Tears welled in her eyes at the lack of airplanes passing by—which was ludicrous, she knew, for she had seen no aircraft flying in quite some time. She shivered, though not from cold, while puffing on her cigarette.

Steve took a drink. "This is eerie."

"Yes. Would you like to take a walk up to the pier?"

"Sure." Steve gave the bottle back to Sally.

They traversed the bicycle path to the stone-walled sandbox at the foot of the pier. The corpses of four children decomposed in the sandbox, recognizable as three boys and a little girl by their clothes and their hair.

They ascended a wooden staircase to the pier. Hundreds of dead bodies littered the promenade, the arcades, the souvenir shops, and the carousel still turning round and round. Other than a few blown bulbs here and there, all of the bright, multicolored lights and beeping video games remained functioning. The dried blood covering the white plastic horses of the carousel was abundant—a shockingly mute reminder that these people had been living lives before the new pneumonic plague made them bleed to death from their nostrils and their mouths.

To their right was Pacific Park, still lit up like a Christmas tree, with its tall unmoving Ferris wheel, and the high motionless roller coaster jutting out over the ocean.

"People used to fish here," Sally said. "Just six weeks ago, and even over a hundred years before, people used to fish from this old pier."

"I know. And they watched these same waves, and danced beneath those same shining stars."

"They shopped for souvenirs." Sally took a drink. "They played volleyball down there on the beach." She gave the bottle to Steve.

He drank. "They dined in all these ocean-view restaurants." He drank again and gave the bottle back.

"I can't take much more of this." Sally swilled deeply from the bottle. "Let's walk down to the shore. I need to hear the indifference of the sea."

They finished their whiskey on the beach, and made love beneath the stars. Afterward, they passed out holding hands.

***

Justin drove around Los Angeles, guzzling bourbon from a bottle, searching for a survivor to consume. He was hungry, and not just any food would do. Justin was in the mood for human flesh.

He had been a killer and a cannibal since his teens, and now that he was pushing forty—and despite the fact that he was a heavy smoker and drinker—he could easily pass for a man ten years younger. His thick dark hair wasn't graying or receding in the least. His face was still fresh and devoid of lines. He had retained his lean physique with only minimal exercise, and in his heart he had lost none of his boyish capacity for wonder.

None of this surprised him. The key to extended youth wasn't a mystery, for when he killed someone and ate them, he absorbed their very essence, their vitality, their life force.

But Yersinia-Z had reduced the smorgasbord of humanity to morsels . . .

Tonight, however, he happened upon a club in East L.A., off the Santa Ana Freeway, in which six Mexican male survivors had gathered. Three sat at a table, engaged in a game of cards. Two played eight ball on a pool table. One stood behind the bar. Their Spanish chatter ceased when Justin walked in with a machine gun slung over his shoulder.

He strolled up to the bar and tossed a fifty on the counter. "Give me a glass of whiskey."

The bartender had thick tattooed forearms, a broad chest, dark eyes, and a bearded face. "You got the fucking plague, man?"

Justin smirked. "Do I look like I'm dying to you?"

"Why the fuck you bringing that gun in here?"

"It's a new world out there," Justin said. "I carry a gun everywhere I go. So, unless you have something against white, Anglo-Saxon, heterosexual males, I would greatly appreciate that glass of whiskey."

The bartender smiled, and Justin shot him eight or nine times in the chest, neck, and face before spinning around and introducing the five remaining patrons to annihilation with a casual spray of gunfire. Then he crossed the club and locked the entrance door.

Justin feasted.

***

Before the plague, Polly Crawford—twenty-two years of age—had been working on her first novel while battling her addiction to alcohol. But now that Yersinia-Z had wiped out most of the planet's population, she saw little logic in stopping drinking anytime soon. Besides, according to the broadcasters on the few radio programs transmitted during the lonely hours of night, the only people still alive were alcoholics.

How ironic was that?

The booze that she had feared would be the death of her was perhaps the one thing keeping her alive.

She was, however, still writing that first novel—despite the fact that there were now no agents or publishers to accept it, no audience to receive it, and almost no one left alive on planet Earth to even read it.

But finishing her book was still important to Polly, for she was curious to see how the story ended. Or at least that's what she told herself this morning while drinking whiskey and stepping over corpses on the shore of the beach at Santa Monica.

The sun was a low yellow orb to the east when she happened upon a young man and a young woman who were still alive but sleeping, half-naked, on the sand. An empty liquor bottle rested at their feet. Two semiautomatic pistols lay within their reach.

Polly—with no desire to be shot—drew her own pistol and clicked the safety off.

She wanted to wake them up, but didn't know what to say, and therefore fired a bullet into the ocean.

That did the trick: both of them opened their eyes immediately.

"Good morning, my fellow survivors," Polly said. "I was beginning to think there was no one around here left alive but the homeless drunks wandering around downtown. I believe their brains are so fried they don't realize that everyone's dead and they can now move into their choice of a thousand mansions."

She introduced herself. Sally and Steve followed suit.

Polly put her gun away. "I apologize for waking you. I'm obviously smashed and starving for conversation."

"All will be forgiven," Sally said, "as long as you strip out of those clothes and share your whiskey."

Steve now sat cross-legged on the shore, and Polly saw his big stiff penis pointing straight up at the sky. "We hope you're into threesomes," he said. "Sally likes to lick pussy as much as I like to fuck."

Smiling, Polly gave the bottle to Sally and got naked.

***

Justin abandoned the car he was driving after it ran out of gas on Sunset Boulevard. His metabolism, as always, was racing on the stored life energies of all the people he had killed and consumed over the years, but it was simply too hot and early in the day to travel very far on foot. Besides, there were numerous stranded vehicles on the road from which to choose.

He selected a late-model SUV because (1) he liked SUVs, (2) the keys were in the ignition, (3) the fuel tank was almost full, and (4) there were no corpses within stinking up the interior.

The engine started without complaint.

He drove south down Harbor Freeway toward Central Los Angeles, searching for a survivor amongst the dead.

Looking for breakfast.

***

After they finished making love on the beach, Sally and Steve offered Polly—who'd been up all night drinking—a place to sleep in the back of their motorhome.

Polly accepted their invitation. How could she refuse? They were the only appealing people she'd encountered in six weeks, since Yersinia-Z.

But the fact that she'd drunkenly fucked them didn't mean she trusted them completely, and though two doors and a long hallway between the lounge area and the bathroom separated the motorhome's cockpit from the back bedroom, Polly clicked her pistol's safety off before locking the door and lying down on the bed.

She heard the engine start and the brakes release, and she stared at that door. A child could kick it in.

Polly was pleasantly smashed, on the verge of passing out, but consciousness wouldn't surrender just yet. It forced her to crawl beneath the bed and hide with her finger on the trigger before falling asleep.

***

Up front, Sally held their bottle of whiskey in the passenger's seat while Steve drove the motorhome eastward. The sun shone so brightly through the windshield that they had to keep their eyes squinted despite the dark sunglasses they wore.

Sally muted the stereo. "I'm glad we met Polly."

Steve nodded. "So am I. She's cool."

"I think she likes us."

"Yes," Steve said, their threesome still vivid in his memory. "If she doesn't, she's one hell of an actress."

"She wasn't faking those orgasms. And I've been thinking that perhaps the three of us should start a family."

"Start a family? You mean, like, stay together?"

"No, silly," Sally said. "I mean that maybe you should get me and Polly pregnant. We could be like Adam and Eve in the Garden of Eden, only with three of us we could multiply more quickly."

Steve laughed. "Honey, this is post-apocalyptic Los Angeles, and we're a long way removed from the Garden of Eden."

Sally lit a cigarette. "It was just a thought. But someone has to begin the process of repopulating this planet. Why not us?"

"Okay," Steve said. "Suppose we *do* make babies. What are we going to do once they're born? Feed them whiskey to keep them from getting Yersinia-Z? Their livers couldn't process the alcohol. They'd be dead before they learned how to walk."

Sally nodded. "You're right. Forget it."

Steve patted her leg. "At least we have each other."

"For now," Sally said, and frowned.

An SUV pulled up next to them at the intersection.

Steve rolled down his window after a man wearing a trench coat got out of the SUV and approached their motorhome.

"Good morning," the man said. "I didn't think there was anyone left in this city alive. I'm Justin. Mind if I climb aboard for a brief discussion?"

"Not at all. I'm Steve. Come on in."

***

Justin entered the motorhome. A woman with Steve introduced herself as Sally. Moments later, the three of them drank whiskey in the lounge area.

Justin—looking around at their hoard of firearms and ammunition—said, "It's best to be prepared, I suppose. For danger has a way of appearing when you least expect it."

He then drew a revolver and shot Steve in the face at pointblank range. The heavy-caliber bullet basically decapitated Steve, and he crashed into the built-in sofa—instantly dead—before sliding off onto the motorhome's carpeted floor.

"Son of a bitch!" Sally screamed, and then lunged at Justin with her bare hands.

He easily overpowered her, eventually knocking her out by slamming his gun's barrel twice against her temple.

Then he taped her mouth shut and bound her hands and feet with some rope he'd been carrying in his trench coat.

He searched the bathroom, the closet, and kicked in the back bedroom's locked door. There was no one else onboard.

Justin drove the motorhome to a mall and parked behind it, then settled down to feast on human flesh.

***

Lying on her stomach beneath the bed, Polly woke up instantly at the sound of gunfire. The single shot was followed by Sally screaming at someone. A brief struggle ensued. Then she heard approaching footsteps out in the hallway.

Polly had been sleeping with her feet toward the headboard, and was therefore facing the bedroom door when, moments later, it was kicked in. She saw a man's black boots and the rumpled ends of his blue jeans straight ahead. She aimed her pistol at his shins, held her breath, and hoped he didn't peer beneath the bed. She would shoot him in the face if he exposed it, but—uncertain of the number of intruders—she didn't want to draw attention to herself in this vulnerable position if he wasn't alone.

Curiously, the man didn't search beneath the bed. Polly watched his feet turn around and walk away. Was he *that* stupid? Why would the door have been locked in the first place if no one occupied this room? Perhaps he had smelled the whiskey vapors seeping from her pores and was toying with her, teasing her like a cat playing with a cornered mouse, creating an illusion of escape when there was none.

She waited, listening, but heard him speak to no one. Moments later, after the motorhome began to move, Polly crawled out from underneath the bed.

Her bladder felt on the verge of bursting. Pistol thrust out before her, she risked a glance into the hallway: it was deserted. Only two steps were necessary to move from the bedroom to the bathroom. Once inside, she sat down on the commode and relieved herself. When finished, she wiped dry with toilet paper, then stood and quickly pulled her pants up.

Suddenly, the motorhome was no longer in motion. After the engine stopped, she parted the curtains to peek out the bathroom window. Whoever was driving had parked behind a shopping mall. Perhaps a thousand corpses decomposed on the asphalt beneath the blind glare of the morning sun.

Polly waited, listening, the pounding of her heart like the ticking of a clock, and she badly needed a shot of whiskey.

Eventually, she could wait no longer. She stepped out of the bathroom, tiptoed down the hallway, and stood at the threshold of the lounge area.

Sally lay roped flat on her back across the coffee table, naked, bleeding from a gash on her temple, mouth taped shut but still very much alive, with bright, wide-open eyes.

The intruder sat likewise naked, on the floor before the sofa, eating Steve's raw flesh with a butcher's knife and bare bloody hands. When he saw Polly standing there pointing a pistol at him, she could tell by his expression that he was baffled by her unforeseen arrival. He tossed aside a piece of dripping meat, and then stood up with a massive erection: his thick penis was longer than his butcher's knife.

He smiled. "You must have been hiding beneath the bed."

"Did you hear that, Sally?" Polly said. "We're dealing with a regular Einstein here."

"For all his genius," the man said, "Einstein died in 1955. He discovered that energy equals mass times the speed of light squared, but he couldn't unlock the secret to eternal life. I, however, am immortal. The flesh, the blood, and the very souls I absorb from my victims will sustain me through eternity."

"You're an idiot with delusions of grandeur," Polly said.

With the hand not holding the butcher's knife, the man clutched his erection. "You mistake my enlightenment for insanity."

Polly cocked her head. "Do you believe in God?"

"No. Of course not."

"Well, I do. And I also believe in Satan. And when you get to Hell, I want you to tell the devil that a female sent you there." She then emptied her clip into the intruder, filling his chest, neck, and face with fifteen rounds of 9mm ammunition, exposing the cannibal's claim of immortality for what it was: a sham; a self-deception.

Polly removed the tape from Sally's mouth and unbound her from the coffee table.

Sally sprang to her feet. "That crazy son of a bitch killed Steve and fucking ate him!"

"I know," Polly said. "But you'll see Steve again, as soon as you're dead."

"How can you be so certain?"

"With faith. Without faith, we're as lifeless as the masses that have perished in the wake of Yersinia-Z."

Sally got dressed. "I wish I shared your optimistic outlook."

Polly shrugged. "It could be worse. At least we have each other."

"For now," Sally said, and frowned.

In the meantime, there was little else to do but guzzle whiskey.

## DEGREES OF SEPARATION

Russell walked out of 36 South Street where he worked for Lawson and Lawson as a stock analyst. He saw the young woman across the street immediately. She was leaning against a lamppost, smoking a cigarette. He had seen her there several times over the past few weeks. Today she wore a short black skirt and a pink tank top that accentuated her breasts. She was beautiful, and appeared to be the same age his daughter would have been had she not been killed ten years before. He had been planning to approach her from the first moment he saw her by the lamppost, but that had been over a month ago, and he still had not worked up the courage to do it.

He watched a car pull up to the corner where she stood. The passenger's-side window slid down. She discarded her cigarette and leaned into the car for a couple of minutes, then stood up again, and the car pulled away.

Russell crossed the street and stopped by the lamppost. The woman looked up at him, but didn't say a word. Suddenly nervous, he cleared his throat. "Young lady, there is something I want you to do for me."

"I may be young," she said, "but I'm no lady. And what took you so long, anyway?"

His nervousness increased, and he wished he had taken a Valium before leaving work. "What do you mean?"

"Never mind," she said. "What is it?"

He ran fingers through his salt-and-pepper hair. "What's what?"

"The thing you want me to do for you. What is it?"

He needed to settle down and get himself together. This was, after all, a business proposition. "Can we go somewhere and talk?"

"Listen," she said. "I'm losing business talking to you. Why don't you come back when you're ready to do some business?"

"I want you to be my daughter for the evening."

She laughed, and her laughter reminded him of his daughter's laughter before she had died. "Do you want me to call you Daddy?"

He nodded. "Yes. Call me Daddy."

"Okay, Daddy." She batted her long eyelashes. "Do you have any money?"

He retrieved a silver money clip from his pocket. He withdrew a few hundred-dollar bills and put them in her palm. "I'll pay you more as we go along."

She put the bills in her purse and hooked her arm through his. "As you wish, Daddy. Lead the way."

They turned and started up the street.

"I had a daughter once," Russell said. "Her name was Patricia. For the rest of the night, I'll call you Patty."

"Thank you for such a lovely name, Daddy. But if you're keeping me for the rest of the night, I'm going to need at least five thousand dollars."

"Fine. There's a bank just up the street. I'll pay you there. Then we need to go shopping and get you some clothes."

***

In the restaurant, conversation hummed over the sporadic clinking of silverware and the clatter of saucers and plates. Russell and Patty sat at a table near the front of the room. The maître d' had spoken to Russell by name when they came in, which he suspected had impressed Patty more than the expensive clothes he had bought for her. The outfit she had been wearing was in the back of his Mercedes in the parking lot.

They ate in silence. After their plates were taken away, they shared a bottle of expensive champagne.

Russell said, “You look ravishing.”

Patty smiled. “Thank you, Daddy. But you still haven’t told me what it is that you want me to do.”

He poured some more champagne in his glass. “I want you to spend the weekend at my house in Dutchess County.”

She smiled and cocked her head. “Where is Dutchess County?”

“About ninety miles north of the city.”

She thought about it. “The whole weekend will cost you another ten thousand dollars.”

“Money isn’t a problem. I have cash in a safe at my house. I’ll pay you when we get there.”

She batted her eyelashes. “Whatever you say, Daddy.”

He smiled. “You’re a wonderful daughter, Patty.”

She looked at his hand. “You’re not wearing a wedding band.”

“No. My wife died ten years ago.”

She licked her lips. “You must be so lonely.”

"Yes. And perhaps you can help me with that. But first, I want you to seduce my son."

"Your son?"

"Yes. That's what I'm paying you for. I want you to seduce my son because you look like his sister."

"I need some air," she said. "You're making me hot and wet."

Russell raised a hand to signal the waiter. "Come on," he said. "Let's get the check and go. I'll tell you all about it on the road."

***

Russell drove.

Just outside of Manhattan, Patty lit a cigarette on the passenger's side. She cracked her window. "Tell me about your son."

Russell turned off the radio. "His name is Jonathan. He's twenty-two."

"Hey," Patty said. "I'm also twenty-two."

"Yes. I thought you looked the same age his sister would have been."

"So they were twins?"

"Yes. Jonathan was born two minutes before Patricia."

"They were very close, weren't they?"

"Yes. Extremely."

"And were they lovers?"

"Yes. How did you guess?"

"That was easy." Patty flipped ashes out the window. "You want me to seduce Jonathan because I look like his sister."

"He hasn't been the same since she died."

"What happened to her?"

"Her mother killed her," Russell said. "She found out they were having sex and it drove her crazy."

Patty discarded her cigarette and closed the window. "When was this?"

"Ten years ago."

"Didn't you say that your wife died ten years ago?"

"Yes. She killed Patricia, and then she killed herself."

From her purse, Patty retrieved a breath mint and put it in her mouth. "Personally, I never understood why people freak out over incest."

"Oh, it wasn't the incest that freaked her out," Russell said. "In fact, she had been molesting Jonathan for years."

"She was fucking her own son?"

"Yes. When she found out that he was also fucking Patricia, she went insane with jealousy. She shot Patricia in the head, then got in bed beside her and blew her brains out. When I came home from work, Jonathan was in bed with them both. He never said a word, and hasn't spoken since."

"Do you ever wonder why she didn't kill Jonathan?"

"We'll never know," Russell said. "She didn't leave a note."

***

Night had fallen when they arrived in Dutchess County. Russell drove her up a long private driveway to his house on a hill overlooking the river. Outdoor lanterns illuminated the property. He parked in a circular drive near the front and killed the engine.

Patty said, "This place is massive."

They got out and entered the house. Russell led Patty to his library. Throughout the spacious chamber, the heads of dead animals gazed at her blindly from the walls.

He gestured to a sofa in one of the armchair-furnished reading areas. "Have a seat."

Patty sat down on the sofa, then looked up into the glass eyes of a bison. "Are you a hunter, Daddy?"

"No. I'm not much of a reader, either. The library was furnished when I bought the house."

"That's too bad," Patty said. "Reading is one of life's greatest pleasures."

"Ah, so you're a literate whore, are you?"

"Don't be mean, Daddy. Books helped me through a lot of troubled times in my youth."

Russell opened a minibar next to the sofa. "Care for something to drink?"

"Yes, please."

"We have wine, whiskey, vodka—"

"Vodka, please," Patty said.

He filled two lowball glasses with vodka, handed one to Patty, and then joined her on the sofa. He raised his glass. "To you," he said. "My daughter, back from the dead."

"To your son," Patty said, "whom I cannot wait to seduce."

They drank.

Russell set his glass on the table. "I need to tell you something about Jonathan."

Patty took another sip. "Fire away."

"He's dangerous."

"So am I," Patty said. "I'm not afraid."

"Maybe you should be."

"Maybe you should take me to meet him."

Russell said, "He's locked up in the basement."

"Are you fucking kidding me?"

"Not at all."

"Why is he locked up in the basement?"

"Because he's violent and he wants to kill me."

"Why does he want to kill you?"

"I don't know. He hasn't spoken a word in over a decade."

"Is he violent with everyone, or only with you?"

Russell shrugged. "I don't know. That's what I want to find out."

Patty finished her drink and stood up. "Take me to meet him."

Russell led her to a bookcase. "Remember those old movies with the mansions that have secret passageways?" He pushed a button concealed behind a copy of *Washington Square* by Henry James. A door disguised to look like part of the wall opened onto a hidden staircase. He turned a light on. "After you."

Patty started down the stairs. Russell closed the door behind them and followed her into the basement.

He led her down a stone-walled hallway. They passed through several steel doors. On the last door, Russell tapped a numerical sequence into a keypad, locking the door behind them. “Jonathan’s homicidal,” he explained. “We can’t let him escape.”

Patty checked her phone. *No signal,* she thought. *Not that I expected one.*

“I hope you don’t have a heart attack down here,” she said. “If something happens to you, I’ll never get out alive.”

They stood in a large bare room with cinderblock walls, a concrete floor, and a ceiling that appeared to be made of steel. One of the walls featured a large window into an adjoining chamber.

“Jonathan’s in there,” Russell said, pointing to the chamber beyond the window.

Patty approached the glass, peering into what looked like the presidential suite of a luxury hotel. She saw Jonathan immediately. He was seated on a sofa, reading a book in the brightly-lit living room. “He’s so beautiful,” she whispered.

“You don’t have to whisper,” Russell said. “He can’t hear us. He can’t see us, either. That window’s made of one-way glass.”

She could not take her eyes off Jonathan. "He looks like a girl."

"Don't be deceived by his appearance. He's stronger than he looks. He could snap your neck in an instant. You can't see it from here, but he has a gym in there. He works out several times per day."

"Let me guess," Patty said. "You have cameras hidden in all of his rooms?"

"Of course. I like to keep an eye on him."

She turned and looked at Russell. "You're a freak."

He smiled. "You have no idea."

"How long has he been in there?"

"Over a decade."

"You never let him out?"

"No. If I did, he would end up in prison. Trust me, he's better off in there."

Patty looked at Jonathan again. "He doesn't look dangerous."

"Tell that to the last girl I hired to seduce him."

"What happened to her?"

"You don't want to know."

Patty looked at Russell. "Why do you want someone to seduce him?"

"Because," Russell said, "I would like to have grandchildren one day. I don't expect you to have a baby with Jonathan, but if I could at least get him having sex with women regularly, it would be a step in the right direction."

"I'll see what I can do," Patty said.

"Excellent." From his jacket, Russell produced a taser and a stun gun. "Do you know what these are?"

"Of course."

"Good. I almost never have to use these on him anymore, but I would never go in there empty-handed." He pressed a button and activated the stun gun. A blue electric arc formed between the two prongs on the top of the device. A loud crackling sound accompanied the blue electric arc. "If Jonathan gets violent, just press this anywhere against his body." He turned the stun gun off and handed it to Patty. "I'll hold on to the taser," he said.

She nodded. "Fine. I'm ready when you are."

There was a steel door next to the one-way window. On the steel door was a keypad. Russell tapped a numerical sequence into the keypad and opened the door. "After you."

Patty entered the chamber.

Russell followed her in, then closed the door behind them and locked it.

On the sofa, Jonathan looked up from his book. His eyes widened. He put the book aside and stood up. “Patricia?”

***

Russell was stunned. It was the first word he had heard his son speak in over a decade.

Patty began weeping. She approached Jonathan and embraced him.

*Great performance,* Russell thought.

Jonathan wrapped his arms around Patty and squeezed. He closed his eyes and buried his face in her hair. “Patricia,” he said. “Oh, Patricia, how I’ve missed you.”

Russell smiled. This was going better than expected. He had hoped that Jonathan would be attracted to the prostitute because she looked like Patricia, but evidently Jonathan really believed that his sister had somehow come back from the dead.

“I suppose I’ll leave you two alone,” Russell said.

Then he turned and headed for the door.

***

Patty released Jonathan. She dropped the stun gun on the floor and pulled a pistol from her purse. Then she turned and pointed the gun at Russell. “Not so fast.”

Russell spun back around and saw the gun aimed at his chest. "Is this a joke?"

"No. And I didn't just happen to be standing by that lamppost. I've been staking out your office at Lawson and Lawson for over a month."

Russell looked at the gun again, and then back into her eyes. "Mind if I ask why?"

"Because I wanted you to lead me to my brother."

"What the hell are you talking about?"

"I'm your daughter," she said. "Patricia."

"That's impossible. My daughter has been dead for over a decade."

"No. Mom didn't kill me, and she didn't kill herself. You caught Mom, Jonathan, and me having sex, and *you* went insane with jealousy. You wanted Jonathan and me all to yourself. But Jonathan was always your favorite. I suppose that's why you decided not to kill him."

"But I killed you."

"No. You broke Mom's neck, but all you managed to do to me was give me whiplash. I pretended to be dead, and you fell for it."

Russell smiled. "You're a cunning little bitch. I'll give you that."

"Thank you. I learned from the best."

"You were still alive when I strapped you in the car."

"Yes. It was dark out. After you put the car in the lake, I climbed out the back window and swam to shore."

"I should have checked for a pulse," Russell said. "That was back when I was drinking way too much. You never would have gotten away with it had I not been drunk."

Patricia smiled. "That's probably true."

"So where have you been all this time?"

"Working the streets. Living with different men. I've been a prostitute since I was twelve years old."

"Why didn't you go to the police?"

She shrugged. "I don't know. At first, I was afraid you'd hurt Jonathan if I did. Plus, going to the police isn't my style. Besides, I like being a prostitute. It satisfies my raving nymphomania. But I've been saving money, and now I have a place of my own. And when I leave here, I'm taking Jonathan with me."

Russell looked at Jonathan, who was staring at the floor, and then returned his gaze to Patricia.

She took her brother's hand, still aiming the gun at her father. "What you never understood is that we enjoyed having sex with our mother. The three of us loved each other deeply. But we all hated you. The sex with you was always outright rape. My earliest memory is being raped by you. According to Mom, you started raping Jonathan and me when we were babies."

"Nonsense," Russell said. "I didn't touch either of you until you were two."

She released her brother's hand. "That's probably why you want grandchildren, so you can rape babies again. But it doesn't matter. Jonathan and I are leaving. Open the door."

"I'm afraid I can't do that."

She took a step closer to her father and aimed the gun at his face.

"You know you can't kill me," Russell said. "I'm the only one who knows the keypad combination."

"True. But I could shoot your kneecaps out first, and then your testicles."

"Okay. Fine. You win." He turned around, entered a numerical sequence into the keypad, and opened the door.

"Go on, Jonathan," Patricia said.

Jonathan stepped out of the basement apartment for the first time in over a decade.

Patricia, still pointing the gun at her father, followed Jonathan out.

Then Russell joined them in the large cinderblock room between the apartment and the hallway. After the door closed behind him, he tapped another sequence into the keypad, locking the door.

Then he shot Patricia with the taser.

The pain was immediate. She felt her muscles freeze, then dropped her gun and fell to the floor. She never lost consciousness, however, and saw her brother attack their father. She wanted to tell Jonathan to stop, that if he killed Russell they would be trapped in this subterranean chamber, but she was incapable of speech.

Jonathan grabbed Russell by the head, then snapped it viciously to the left and broke his neck, killing him instantly.

Patricia screamed. The sound of her father's neck breaking was the same sound her mother's neck had made when he broke it over a decade ago.

Jonathan dropped Russell to the floor. The taser fell out of Russell's hand. The two conductive wires from the taser were still attached to the probes embedded in Patricia's chest.

She watched Jonathan approach her. He got down on his knees and ripped open her dress. The two taser barbs were lodged perhaps an eighth of an inch in her chest. He grabbed the dartlike electrodes, removed them from her flesh, and tossed them aside. "I love you, Patricia," he whispered.

She stood up. The pain was gone and her chest was barely bleeding.

She approached her father. Knowing he was dead, she checked for a pulse nevertheless. She didn't find one.

Then she looked at her brother. "We are trapped."

He said her name: "Patricia."

She went to the steel door between the empty chamber they were trapped in and the stone-walled hallway beyond. She tried to open the door, but it wouldn't budge. She looked at the keypad and thought about infinity.

She turned to Jonathan. "I don't suppose you know the combination, do you?"

He smiled and said her name again: "Patricia."

It occurred to her that perhaps her brother was brain-damaged. Or maybe he was just heavily medicated. Who knew how much abuse Russell had inflicted upon him during the past ten years?

She went to the only other door in the chamber—the door beside the one-way window to Jonathan's apartment. At least in the apartment they would have food and water. Out here, they had nothing.

She tried to open the door, but it was locked.

She picked her pistol up off the floor. "Cover your ears."

Jonathan did.

She fired a couple of rounds into the keypad, and then tried to open the door again, but it wouldn't budge. She went to the other door and repeated the process. Again, her efforts were unsuccessful.

She checked her phone. There was still no signal, and the battery was almost dead. She tossed it aside.

She knew she had eight bullets left, but checked them anyway. Yes: one in the chamber, and seven in the magazine. "Go get in the corner," she said. "Keep your ears covered and stay as close to the floor as possible."

Jonathan followed her instructions.

She aimed her gun at the one-way window. *Please,* she thought, and fired.

Nothing happened.

She fired five more times: not even a crack. Just as she had suspected, the one-way window was made of bulletproof glass.

She joined her brother in the corner and sat down beside him on the floor. She looked around. They were entombed in a grave of concrete, steel, cinderblock, and bullet-resistant glass. No one knew they were there, and no one would be coming to their rescue.

They could survive on their father's corpse for a few days, but what would be the point? They didn't have a drop of water to drink.

Jonathan put his head on her shoulder. "Patricia," he whispered. Then he took her hand.

She thought about all the money she had saved the past few years, and the place she had made for them to be together. "I'm sorry I failed you, brother. All I wanted to do was take you away."

He squeezed her hand, and again whispered her name.

*Two rounds left,* she thought. *One for Jonathan, and one for me.*

But not yet, she decided. She would save the bullets for when their suffering became unbearable.

"I love you, brother. From now on, we'll always be together."

They held each other closely in the silence of their grave.

## THE BOX

Young Bethany, twisting and turning in her highchair, looked up at Judith. "Want some, Mommy?"

Judith forced a smile as Jim attempted to get another spoonful of cereal into their daughter's mouth. "No thank you," Judith said. "Mommy's already eaten. Finish your breakfast."

A noise out in the hallway beyond their apartment door made Bethany look away. At almost two years of age, she was easily distracted by nearly anything. Then she reached a hand out for her cup and knocked it onto the floor. Spilled milk splashed across the linoleum.

"Great," Jim said.

Judith said, "Do you want me to finish feeding her?"

Jim shook his head. "No. It's almost time for you to go to work."

Jim—a writer—worked at home, which eliminated their need for a babysitter.

Judith checked the time on her phone. "I am *so* ready for vacation."

Jim looked up from where he was wiping spilled milk off the floor. "Me too. Just a few more weeks."

Judith leaned down and kissed him. "I'd better go."

"Okay, baby. I love you."

"I love you too." She left.

***

Judith was in the breakroom when her phone rang. It was Jim. She answered on the second ring. "Hi, baby."

"Judith? Oh my god, Judith. Bethany's gone."

***

Judith rushed home. The apartment was a madhouse when she got there. After the police left, she and Jim found themselves on the living-room sofa with the TV off. Now that everyone else was gone, the silence was oppressive, and Judith's anxiety was making her hyperventilate.

Jim appeared to be in shock. He was drinking from a bottle of whiskey and Judith could see that he was already drunk.

"You think it's my fault," Jim said.

"I didn't say that."

"You don't have to. I can see the blame in your eyes."

Judith could think of little to ask Jim that the police had not already asked him. He had spent the morning writing like he always did, and when he checked on Bethany around noon, their daughter was gone. The door to the apartment had been unlocked. Judith couldn't remember if she had locked the door when she left for work or not. Evidently one of two things had happened: either Bethany had wandered out of the apartment on her own, or someone else had come inside and snatched her.

"What time did you start drinking?" Judith said.

Jim shrugged. "I don't know. Not long after you left, I guess. But I wasn't drinking much. I didn't start drinking heavily until after she was already gone."

"And you never heard anything?"

Jim shook his head. Then he took a drink. "I had the TV on for Bethany, but that was low volume. Other than that, I never heard a thing."

Judith ran fingers through her hair. "My god, this is a fucking nightmare."

She looked down at Bethany's box of crayons and coloring book on the coffee table.

***

Judith couldn't sleep. Where on Earth was Bethany? Was she even still alive? She imagined her daughter somewhere out there in the night being raped and tortured by a maniac. She shuddered, hoping her anxiety wouldn't cause a massive heart attack.

Jim was passed out next to her on the bed, reeking of whiskey. Judith checked her phone. The time was 1:06 a.m. She didn't have to be back at work until Monday. She decided to go for a drive and try to calm her mind.

She got up, got dressed, and put some shoes on. She grabbed her car keys. Then she left the apartment and took off down the hallway.

Another apartment door opened and a woman stuck her head out. She appeared to be a decade older than Judith. Thirty or so. Maybe thirty-five. And still highly attractive. "Excuse me," the woman said. "I know you lost your little girl."

Judith nodded. "Yes. My daughter is missing. Did the police speak to you?"

"No. I don't even live here. I'm just keeping watch on this place for a friend. But I can help you find your little girl."

"You can?"

"Yes. But you will have to do me three favors first."

"What are you talking about?"

"I'm talking about you doing three favors for me if you ever want to see your daughter again."

A sickening anger bloomed inside of Judith. "What do you mean? Do you know where Bethany is?"

"Yes, I do."

Adrenaline shot through Judith and suddenly she was close to the woman's face. "Then tell me where she is! Tell me where Bethany is right this instant!"

"Calm down. She isn't here. I can get her back for you, but you have to do those three favors for me first."

"Is this a ransom demand, or something? Are you blackmailing me?"

"You need to calm down and accept what I am offering if you ever want to see your daughter again."

Judith said, "I'm going to the police."

The woman shrugged. "If you do, you will never see your daughter again. You can't go to the police, and you can't speak to your husband about any of this. If you do, I will know. Then I will simply go away, and your daughter will die. The choice is yours, of course, but this is your only chance to save your daughter."

"Okay," Judith said. "What do I have to do?"

The woman smiled. "Three favors. The first one's easy. The second and third? Not so much." The woman stepped back from the open doorway. "But first, come on in. There's something you'll need to take with you from inside the box."

"The box?"

The woman nodded. "Yes. Come on in. You'll see."

Judith stepped into an empty room. There was no furniture or anything else other than a wooden box in the center of the room on the hardwood floor. The box was about the size of a laundry basket.

"Open the box," the woman said.

Judith did. Inside the box was only a single silver key. "Looks like a house key."

"It is. Put it in your pocket."

Judith did.

Then the woman gave her an address and told her what the first favor would be.

***

Judith parked her car in front of the old man's house and turned off the engine. It was almost two a.m. and there was no traffic on the residential street. She got out and approached the house.

*He's very old and bedridden,* the woman had told her. *He probably won't even be awake. If he is awake, he certainly won't give you any problems. Just tell him you're one of his nurses and you need to check his medication. He keeps the journal in the nightstand beside his bed. It's a hardback journal. Black. You can't miss it. Just grab the journal, leave, and bring it here to me. If you don't, your daughter will die. If you do, you'll only have two favors left to do for me. That key in your pocket unlocks the front door, and there is no alarm. You have two hours.*

Judith's hands were shaking when she got to the front door. *Calm down,* she told herself. *Just focus on Bethany.* She took the key from her pocket, unlocked the door, and opened it. She took a deep breath. Then she stepped inside.

A foul smell greeted her immediately.

She crossed a living room. She passed a kitchen on her left and a bathroom on her right. There was a light on in a room with an open door at the end of a hallway. Judith approached the room and stepped inside.

It was the old man's bedroom. The man was dead. He had been slaughtered and dismembered. His body had been hacked into perhaps thirty pieces and there was blood all over the walls, the floor, and the bed. His severed head rested upright on a pillow at the top of his mutilated body.

Judith took her shoes off and left them on the floor by the door. She crossed the room and took the journal from the nightstand where the woman had told her it would be. Then she put her shoes back on and left.

***

The woman opened the door. "That was fast."

Judith handed her the journal. "The man had been decapitated and hacked to pieces. Why didn't you just take the journal yourself when you murdered him?"

The woman smiled briefly. Then she gave Judith a look that sent chills up and down her spine. "We wanted you to see what will happen to your daughter if you refuse to do the second favor. Be here tomorrow at noon and I'll tell you what you have to do."

***

Judith woke up. She brushed her teeth and went into the kitchen.

Jim sat at the table, talking on his phone. "Yes. Of course. I see. Okay. Thank you. Goodbye." He put the phone down and looked up at Judith. "There's nothing new. They said they'll call us if they hear anything."

Judith retrieved a soda from the refrigerator and opened it.

"They may do a press conference later," Jim said.

Judith took a drink. "Okay."

"I think I'll go to the park today," Jim said. "Maybe do some writing there. You know, just to get out of the apartment."

Judith sighed with relief. She had to go see the woman at noon to find out what the second favor would be. "Good idea. I may go to the mall and do some shopping."

Soon thereafter, Jim grabbed his laptop. "See you later."

Judith nodded.

He left.

Judith wondered if they would ever recover from this. Even if they got Bethany back, their lives had been irreversibly damaged.

At noon, she went to the apartment down the hallway. The door was already open and the woman stood in the doorway. "Come on in," the woman said. Judith did. As before (excluding them), there was nothing else in the room but the wooden box.

"Open the box," the woman said.

Judith did. There was a gun inside the box. The gun was a revolver.

"It's a loaded thirty-eight," the woman said. "Take it out."

Judith did.

"Do you know how to shoot a gun?"

Judith nodded. "Yes."

"Good," the woman said. "Because today, you'll have to kill someone."

"Kill someone?"

"Yes. But don't worry. He lives alone, and that gun is untraceable." She gave Judith a name and an address. "We told him you were coming, so he'll be expecting you. He'll think it's a business visit. Kill him today, but don't get rid of the gun. Just kill him today, go home, and then come back here tomorrow."

"Same time tomorrow?"

"Yes. Be here at noon."

Judith headed for the door.

"One more thing," the woman said.

Judith turned around. "What is it?"

"We'll know if you fail to kill him, of course. And if you fail to kill him, your daughter will end up like the man you saw last night."

Judith nodded. "I'll see you tomorrow." She left.

***

The man lived in a small house at the end of a narrow lane. Judith parked her car in his driveway behind a truck and killed the engine. She got out. The day was warm. She didn't see anyone else around. She tucked the gun into the waistband of her jeans at the small of her back and approached the house. She had never killed anyone before. *This is for Bethany,* she told herself. *Any mother would do what I'm about to do.* She took a deep breath, and then she pressed the doorbell.

Moments later, a man opened the door. He smiled. "You must be Judith."

She retrieved the gun and aimed it at his face. "I'm so sorry." Then she pulled the trigger and shot him between the eyes. The .38 slug blew his brains out the back of his head, killing him instantly.

Judith walked back to her car and drove away.

***

The next day, the woman opened the apartment door at noon before Judith could even knock. "Excellent work," the woman said. "You're only one more favor away from seeing your daughter. Come on in."

Judith stepped into the empty room and closed the door behind her.

"Do you still have the gun?"

Judith nodded.

"Great," the woman said. "You may need it later." Then she turned and pointed at the box behind her. "Now you need to open the box and take out what's inside."

Judith approached the wooden box and opened it. Inside the box was a hacksaw. She grabbed the hacksaw by its handle and pulled it out.

"To see your daughter again," the woman said, "the third favor you'll need to do is bring me your husband's head."

"What?"

"Saw your husband's head off, bring it here, and put it inside that box. Otherwise, your daughter's head goes in the box."

"You're insane."

"The choice is yours, Judith."

"Why are you doing this to us?"

"Because your husband lied to me."

"Lied to you?"

"Yes. He told me that he was going to leave you and be with me, but now he says that he's going to stay with you."

"So you've been having an affair with my husband?"

"Yes. For over a year now."

"I don't believe you."

The woman looked into Judith's eyes. Then she told her some intimate details about her husband and Judith knew that it was true.

***

Jim was pointing a gun at Judith when she stepped into the kitchen. In his other hand, he held a hacksaw.

Judith was still holding her own hacksaw, but the revolver was in the waistband of her jeans at the small of her back. "So she struck the same deal with you?" Judith said.

Jim said, "What are you talking about?"

"Three favors to see our daughter again."

Jim nodded, but he looked confused. "Three favors, yes. But it was a man, not a woman. It was the man you've been having an affair with. And don't try to deny it. He told me things about you that he otherwise could not have possibly known."

"Unbelievable," Judith said. "It was a woman who struck the deal with me. The woman *you've* been having an affair with. And apparently, the two of them are working together."

"I stole a journal," Jim said, "and then I killed a woman. Those were the first two favors. What about you?"

"The same," Judith said. "Except I had to kill a man instead of a woman. Now I'm supposed to saw your head off and put it in a box."

Still pointing the gun at Judith, Jim looked down at her hacksaw. Then he held his own hacksaw up. "Same here. This is insane." He set the gun on the kitchen table. Then he picked up his bottle of whiskey and took several drinks. "Why do you think they're doing this?"

Judith shrugged. "I don't know. Maybe they're married, and they both found out that the other was cheating, and they decided to punish us instead of each other. Or maybe they're just evil. Who knows?"

Jim took a few more drinks. "And now one of us has to put the other's head in a box to get our daughter back."

"Maybe there's another way," Judith said, "now that we know what we're up against."

"No," Jim said. "One of us has to die. And since I'm an alcoholic, it should be me. Bethany needs her mother. Show her my picture from time to time, and make sure she knows that I loved her." He raised the hacksaw to his throat.

"Jim! No! Wait!"

He slashed his throat open with the hacksaw's blade, cutting deeply all the way across his neck. Blood shot out of his carotid artery and his jugular vein, and he dropped to the floor in a spreading pool of blood. He made a few gurgling sounds while quickly bleeding out, and then he died.

Judith set her hacksaw on the kitchen table. Then she dropped to her knees and wept. After the tears stopped, her only thoughts were of Bethany. She readied herself for what needed to be done.

She decapitated her dead husband in silence, using Jim's hacksaw instead of her own. She grabbed a heavy-duty black trash bag from beneath the kitchen sink and put the severed head in that.

A phone call to the police would have to wait. Then she changed her mind and decided that she would just drive Bethany to the police station right after she got her back, so that her daughter wouldn't have to see her father's decapitated corpse on the kitchen floor.

Judith took Jim's head to the apartment down the hallway. The door was closed. She knocked, but no one answered. The door was unlocked. She opened it and went inside.

The room was empty except for the wooden box, and she approached it. There was a note on top that was not addressed to anyone: *Put the head on the floor and open the box to see your daughter.*

Judith set the trash bag on the floor. She opened the box. Her daughter's severed head was in the box.

She closed the box and retrieved the revolver. Then she put the barrel in her mouth and pulled the trigger.

## HOME INVASION

The doorbell rang. Marian put down her cup of coffee. Her husband had just left for work about two minutes ago. Had David perhaps forgotten his keys and locked himself out of the house? She left the kitchen, crossed the living room, and opened the front door.

It was not her husband. It was the same large man who had rung the doorbell yesterday morning. When she'd answered it yesterday, he had introduced himself as Simon and claimed to be a landscaper looking for work. Now, as before, she noticed how his eyes kept peering over her shoulders and looking around at the interior of the house. She had neglected to tell David about the man stopping by yesterday because it hadn't seemed like a big deal. Now it did.

"Look," Marian said. "Simon, right?"

He smiled, but there was no warmth in it. "You remember me."

Of course she remembered him. The guy stood about six-five and had to weigh two-fifty at least.

Marian nodded. "Listen, I already told you that we don't need any landscaping services, so you can stop bothering us now."

"Oh," Simon said, "I haven't even begun to bother you yet." Then he forced himself inside and knocked her out.

***

Marian woke up on her bed with a headache. Simon had punched her on the side of her head and she thought she was probably bleeding. She tried to raise a hand to her head but couldn't because her arms were secured to the bedposts. She attempted to slide her wrists out of the handcuffs, but the struggle was useless. "Please," she said. "Just let me go and I won't say anything."

Simon, propping himself up on one arm between her legs, reached out and grabbed her chin. "Let you go? I don't think so." Then he smiled. "We haven't even begun."

Marian started crying. She hated herself for it and the tears made her vision blurry, but she couldn't help it.

Simon leaned back on his knees with his legs folded beneath him. He let go of her chin and put both hands flat on his thighs, staring at her robe. Then he grabbed the robe and yanked it open, exposing her breasts.

*He's going to rape me,* Marian thought. *He's going to rape me and then he's going to kill me. And he'll probably torture me before he kills me.* Still crying, she pulled her eyes away from his hands and looked up at the ceiling.

She heard a metallic sound in front of her. She looked at Simon and saw that he was now holding a knife. The teeth on the bottom of the blade were shiny in the sunlight streaming through the window.

Simon lowered the knife to her stomach. He slid the blade's tip from her navel down to her panties.

"My husband," Marian said.

Simon grinned. "What about him?"

"My husband will be back any minute and he will beat the fucking shit out of you."

It wasn't true, of course. David wouldn't be home for another eight hours or so, but Marian was desperate. And if Simon believed her, maybe he wouldn't do whatever it was he was about to do.

Simon threw his head back and laughed. Then he put his head back down and looked into her eyes. "I watched your husband leave yesterday. Watched him come home, too. He won't be back until sometime after five. And even if he *does* come home early, trust me: I'm not worried about your tiny little husband."

Marian began crying again. Simon was right. David would not be able to help her. Even if he walked in right now, he would be unable to stop this. It was possible that he wouldn't even try. They didn't love each other anymore and had recently been talking about getting divorced. Besides, David was too small to be a physical threat to this behemoth of a man.

Simon reached out with the hand not holding the knife. He grabbed one of her breasts and squeezed it. "I like how your tits jiggle when you cry. Anyone ever tell you that you have nice titties? Yeah, I bet you hear that all the time."

His touch sent shockwaves of revulsion through her body, and she shuddered.

Simon smiled. "You like that, don't you?"

Marian shook her head. "No. Please—"

"Yes you do. You like it when Simon pinches those perky nipples."

Marian closed her eyes.

Simon ran his hand down her stomach and grabbed the top of her panties. Then he paused. “What was that?”

Marian opened her eyes. “What was what?”

“I thought I heard something.”

Marian cocked her head and listened, but she didn’t hear anything.

Simon must have thought that he hadn’t heard anything either, because he ripped her panties off and grinned. “Shaved,” he said. “I like that.”

Marian went rigid and closed her eyes. Then she heard a loud thud and opened them. She saw a dazed expression on Simon’s face before his own eyes rolled back in his head. Then he fell off the bed and crashed onto the floor.

David stood at the foot of the bed. He held a golf club over one shoulder like a baseball bat. “You’re a goddamn whore.”

Marian blinked a couple of times. “What are you talking about?”

“I got all the way to work and realized I’d forgotten my phone. Left it on charge again. So I come home to get it and find you in bed with a goddamn Sasquatch.”

"Jesus Christ, David! He was going to rape me! And probably kill me! Didn't you see the knife in his hand? You just saved my life."

"Yeah, right. You expect me to believe that bullshit?"

"It's true! He broke in here right after you left for work."

"There's no sign of a forced entry. As a matter of fact, the door was locked when I got here."

"He rang the doorbell. I opened the door. That's when he forced his way inside."

"So you answered the door in your robe?"

"Jesus Christ, David! You had just left for work! I was still drinking my first cup of coffee! And he had already stopped by yesterday morning. Scoping the place out, apparently. Said he was a landscaper named Simon looking for work."

"You didn't tell me about anyone stopping by yesterday morning."

"I didn't think it was a big deal."

David shook his head. "You know what I think? I think every word out of your mouth is a goddamn lie."

Marian rolled her eyes. "If you haven't noticed, David, I'm in *fucking handcuffs* here. The son of a bitch forced his way in, knocked me out, and handcuffed me to the bed."

"Bullshit. I don't see any blood or bruises on you anywhere. And I know you like to watch all kinds of kinky porn, because you never delete your search history. You probably like it when old Sasquatch ties you up." David looked down at the large, unconscious man on the floor. "Or Simon. Whatever the fuck his name is."

Marian shook her head. "You're unbelievable. But anyway, he probably has the keys in his pocket. So will you please get me out of these handcuffs?"

David bent down beside the bed. He didn't search Simon's pockets for any keys, however. Instead, he dragged Simon out of the bedroom by his legs.

He was gone for quite some time. When he returned to the bedroom a little while later, David sat down on the bed beside Marian and fired up his crack pipe.

"I thought you quit smoking crack," Marian said.

David ignored her. He just sat on the edge of the bed and smoked in silence.

"Is Simon dead?" Marian said.

David shook his head. "Nope. He's just unconscious. He's bleeding from the back of his head, but he's still breathing."

"Jesus Christ, David. What if he wakes up?"

"Then I'll knock him out again. And don't worry: Simon won't be moving around anytime soon. I found some rope out in the garage and tied him up in the spare bedroom."

"Did you find the keys to the handcuffs?"

David ignored her. He took his phone from his pocket and placed a call.

"Are you calling the police?"

David spoke into the phone. "HR, please." Moments later: "Joy? Hi. This is David. I left work a little bit ago to come home and take some medicine, but it's not working. So I won't be back today. I'm just gonna stay home all weekend recuperating, and then I'll be back as good as new on Monday morning. Yes. Thank you. Yes. I will. Okay. You too. Thanks again. Goodbye." He put the phone back in his pocket.

"Aren't you going to call the police?"

David hit his crack pipe several times. Then he lit a cigarette. "Don't worry: I'll call the police later to report that you were murdered."

"Murdered?"

"Yes. Later, when I'm ready, I'll bring Simon back in here. I'll kill you first, and then I'll kill him. I'll say I took my medication and passed out. When I woke up, Simon was in the process of killing you. I tried to save you. I attacked him with the golf club, but by the time I got him to stop, you were already dead."

"You'll never get away with it."

"Of course I will. And then I'll start a new life with the money from your life-insurance policy."

The sound of Simon's voice startled them both. "There's only one problem with your plan," Simon said. He stood in the bedroom doorway, holding a rope. "You should have made those knots a whole lot tighter."

Marian was not surprised. Thoroughness had never been one of her husband's strong suits.

"Motherfucker," David said. He reached for his golf club, which was leaning against the nightstand, but Simon attacked him before he could rise from the bed. David put up a struggle, but it was brief and ineffective. Simon was simply too big, too fast, and too strong. He took David to the floor. Marian couldn't see it, but she heard him begin beating David to death.

David's screams turned to whimpers of pain that quickly began to fade. Then all Marian heard were the wet sounds that Simon made as he continued battering her husband's corpse.

Finally, he stopped. There was silence. Then: "Ah, there's my knife." She heard him pick it up off the floor, and then he climbed onto the bed.

"Now," Simon said. "Where were we?"

Marian closed her eyes, but he forced them open.

# THE BLACK YACHT

Jessica woke up on the sofa.

"Mommy," Caitlyn said, "can we go to the beach today?"

"I can't talk right now," Jessica said. "Mommy's sick." She sat up and tied some plastic around her arm. A blue vein rose. She grabbed a syringe and injected herself with heroin.

Almost instantly, she was better. Cured. No longer dopesick. "What were you saying, Caitlyn?"

The six-year-old looked out the window. "Can we go to the beach today? I want to look for seashells."

"Yes," Jessica said. "I need to find more medicine, anyway."

They left.

***

The sand was white in the sun's glare. The sea scattered the shells of dead and dying creatures on the shore. The beach wasn't too crowded, but there were still quite a few people tanning, looking at their phones, and eating snacks on blankets and beach towels.

Holding a folded blanket, Jessica headed north along the shore. Caitlyn walked beside her, picking up seashells and putting them in the plastic bucket she carried.

Jessica scanned the faces of all the people they passed, but she didn't see anyone who looked like they might be selling heroin. She still had some left, but she was running low, and she needed to get more soon or she would be in trouble.

They came to a less-populated stretch of sand. Jessica unfolded her blanket and sat down facing the sea. Caitlyn walked down to the surf.

Jessica injected herself with heroin. After that, she kept slipping in and out of consciousness.

Sometime later, she heard the deep smooth voice of a man say: "How much for the little girl?"

Jessica opened her eyes and looked up, squinting against the sun. She saw the shape of a tall man, but she couldn't see his face. She sat up.

"How much for the little girl?" the man repeated.

Now she could see him clearly. Strikingly handsome, he was not dressed for the beach at all. His flesh was pale, and his eyes were blue. He wore black pants, a black shirt, and a long black coat. His long black hair was pulled back in a ponytail. Jessica got the impression of great wealth and gentility.

"My daughter's not for sale," Jessica said. "Unless, of course, you happen to have a lifetime supply of china white."

"China white?"

"Heroin."

The man smiled. His teeth were perfect. "I have not heard heroin referred to as china white for many years. These days, china white can mean different things. I do, however, happen to have an abundance of heroin in my boat." He nodded out to sea at a yacht in the distance. The large boat—a billionaire's vessel—was as black as his clothes and his hair.

He pulled a phone from his pocket and keyed in a number. Then he spoke into the phone: "Bring me a briefcase of heroin." He disconnected and put the phone back in his pocket.

"Two associates," the man told Jessica, "will be riding over from my yacht on a smaller boat."

To their left, Caitlyn was building a sandcastle. She wasn't paying them any attention whatsoever.

Soon thereafter, two men arrived on a four-person, motor-driven dinghy. The small boat stopped a few feet from the shore. One of the men stayed on the boat. The other man got out and walked onto the sand with a briefcase. He put the briefcase down without saying a word and then returned to the boat.

The man picked up the briefcase and opened it.

Jessica looked inside the briefcase. It was full of heroin.

"All of this," the man said, "for an afternoon on my yacht with your daughter. And then I'll return her to you in one piece sometime later this evening."

"In one piece?"

He nodded. "Yes. In one piece. I give you my word."

Jessica said, "You have yourself a deal."

***

Jessica spent the day on her blanket, clutching the briefcase. She drifted in and out of consciousness. She would wake up, look out at the black yacht in the distance, then get high and nod off again. Sometime after dusk, however, with the stars of twilight sparkling, she looked out to the spot where the boat had remained motionless all day and saw that it was gone.

*Where's my daughter?* Jessica thought.

Then she saw her. Caitlyn lay naked on the beach only a few yards away. But Caitlyn was different now. Horribly, grotesquely different.

Jessica approached her daughter.

*Yes,* the man had said. *In one piece. I give you my word.*

Well, the man had certainly returned her in one piece. But Caitlyn had been drastically rearranged.

Caitlyn lay flat on her stomach. Her head and neck had been severed at the shoulders and reattached at the center of her back. Her arms had been amputated and reattached to the body at the hips. Her legs had been chopped off and were now connected to the shoulders. She looked like a four-legged spider with a human head sticking up out of its back.

And yet there were no stitches, or signs of cutting, or even any drops of blood anywhere on her body. How was that possible?

*It's not,* Jessica thought. *I must be either dreaming or hallucinating.*

Also impossible was the fact that her daughter was still alive. Her eyes were open and she was staring at the sea.

"I don't like the way the world looks anymore," Caitlyn said. "Can we go home now?"

Clutching the briefcase, Jessica nodded, but her daughter didn't see her because she was still looking at the ocean. "Yes," Jessica said. "Let's go home."

Caitlyn's four limbs raised her torso from the sand and lifted it into the air. Then, with her head sticking up out of her back (and keeping both of her eyes closed), she followed her mother to the car, relying on sound instead of sight.

Caitlyn kept her eyes closed the whole way home.

***

The ringing of the phone woke Randy at six a.m., and now he couldn't believe what his ex-wife told him. "You sold our daughter's body for heroin?" he said.

"Yes!" Jessica said. "But that's not even the point! The man wasn't even human!"

Randy lit a cigarette. Then he spoke into the phone again: "What are you talking about?"

"He turned her into a monster who can kill you just by looking at you!" Jessica said. "I'm hiding out in the kitchen right now beneath a blanket, but if she sees me, I'm going to die!"

*Oh, you're going to die all right,* Randy thought. "You're high," he said. "You're high and you're not making any sense."

"He must have been the devil," Jessica said.

"Who?"

"The man with the black yacht. The man I made the deal with. Apparently, I made a deal with the devil. The devil gave me heroin, but he turned our daughter into a monster."

"Stay put," Randy said. "I'm coming over there." He hung up the phone and finished his cigarette. He brushed his teeth, got dressed, and put on a pair of gloves.

Then he grabbed a gun from the collection of guns in his closet. The gun he selected was untraceable. It was also fitted with a silencer. He had bought it from a stranger on the street. The serial number had been filed down before he purchased it. The gun would leave no incriminating trail after he blew Jessica's brains out, but after he killed her he would go ahead and throw it in the river anyway. He shoved the gun into the waistband of his jeans, put his shoes on, and went outside. The cool air revived him. It was dawn and the sun was rising.

He got in his car and headed to Jessica's apartment, deciding that when he got there he would get his daughter, put her in the car, and go back inside and kill his ex-wife. Then he would toss the gun into the river and take Caitlyn home with him. When the cops came asking him questions, he would tell them that when he went to pick Caitlyn up, Jessica had told him to hurry up because one of her many junkie boyfriends was coming over.

He parked in front of Jessica's building and got out. He looked up at the window of her living room on the second floor and thought that the window looked . . . *wrong* somehow. Elongated and misshapen. Then again, maybe he was just tired. Randy wasn't accustomed to being awake this early in the morning.

He went inside and walked up to the second floor. The hallway was quiet. He walked down to apartment 7B and saw that the wooden door was warped. *What the fuck?* He grabbed the knob and twisted it. The door was unlocked. He pushed it open and stepped inside.

The living room was a canvas of insanity, as if some mad artist had gone crazy with a paintbrush and made reality more surreal than anything Randy had ever seen. Everything in the room was . . . *impossible,* altered beyond Randy's comprehension.

The sofa—a black sectional that took up two walls—was arched upward like a mine shaft's entrance, its dripping leather hanging in mid-cascade like a frozen waterfall. The coffee table was now a knotted rope of wood maybe twenty feet long. Half of the loveseat had melted down into the hardwood floor and become part of its surface; the other half had bloomed into something that resembled a Venus flytrap.

Everything on the walls—picture frames, canvases, mirrors, candleholders—had stretched and blended into one another like colors mixed together on a palette.

The window frame was no longer rectangular. It had shifted into a shape that reminded Randy of a malformed starfish. Amazing to him was the fact that the glass panes weren't cracked. Somehow they had flowed seamlessly into their new shapes, as if custom-made to fit the altered frame.

And then he saw Winston on the wall above the loveseat. Or *in* the wall, rather. Winston, Caitlyn's little French Bulldog, had been her pet for the past three years, since she was three, and now he was just a part of the wall. His body had been pulled horizontally along the wall, but his head was about three feet higher than his body, because his neck had been stretched vertically, making him look like a tan brontosaurus.

Tears began to form in Randy's eyes. Caitlyn had loved Winston more than anything.

"Crazy, isn't it?" Jessica said.

Randy turned around. His ex-wife—with a blanket wrapped around her body—stood facing him at the threshold of the kitchen.

"The devil changed her," Jessica said, "and now Caitlyn changes everything she looks at. I don't even think she means to do it. So far, this blanket has protected me. Whenever she comes around, I cover myself with the blanket. If she can't see me, she can't change me."

Randy pulled the gun from the waistband of his jeans. "This is insane."

"Yes," Jessica said. "The devil turned our daughter into a monster."

"No," Randy said. "You're a monster who sold our daughter for heroin."

He raised the gun and shot her through the head, killing her instantly. Brains and blood blew out the back of her skull and her body hit the floor.

"Daddy?"

He turned to the left and looked down. His daughter was looking up at him from the floor. She looked like a big white spider with Caitlyn's head sticking up out of its back. "Dear God," Randy said.

And then there was pain.

***

Caitlyn couldn't stop what was happening. Her father was changing just like everything else she looked at, so instead of looking away, she just watched.

Smoke started pouring out of his ears, nose, and mouth. His head dissolved. His limbs liquefied. His torso melted down to the floor. Then, as if the floor were a tilted dinner plate, her father's remains traveled to the nearest wall like a puddle of mercury. Then the puddle ascended to the ceiling. It moved across the ceiling to the middle of the room before it began to drip. It froze about halfway to the floor and hung like a pink stalactite. Her father's face was visible near the tip. His eyes appeared to watch her like the eyes of a painting in a haunted house.

Caitlyn looked away, sad, but suddenly famished.

Her mother never kept much food in the apartment, and Caitlyn had already eaten all of the cereal and crackers in the cupboards. Her mother's brains and blood smelled awfully appetizing, however.

She crab-walked over to her mother's corpse and began to feed.

## SIREN SONG

Friday night. Two young women in a nightclub—a blonde and a brunette.

"Oh my god," the brunette said. "He's looking at you."

"Who?"

"That guy over there in the corner with the long black hair."

The blonde looked. Sure enough, the man was looking at her. "He's kind of cute."

"Don't you recognize him?"

"No."

"You must not be from around here."

"I'm not," the blonde said.

"What's your name, sweetie?"

"Heidi."

"Nice to meet you, Heidi. Anyway, that man over there is either Liam or Alec Roth. Identical twins. Can't tell them apart. The Roth family has more money than God."

Heidi glanced over at the man again. He was still staring at her. He looked to be about the same age as most of the people in the club: early twenties. He was dressed in casual clothes. "If he's so rich," Heidi said, "what's he doing in a place like this?"

The woman shrugged. "Probably trying to get laid like everyone else." She walked away.

Heidi sipped her drink.

The man got up from his table and approached her. "I've never seen you in here before. I'm Liam. What's your name?"

"Heidi."

"You're not from Boston."

She smiled. "That obvious, huh?"

"Your accent," he said. "Kentucky? Tennessee?"

Heidi sipped her drink. "West Virginia."

"Beautiful state," Liam said. "I go there to paint landscapes occasionally."

"You're an artist?"

He nodded.

"So am I," Heidi said. "That's why I came to Boston. To go to art school."

Liam sipped his drink. "I want to paint your portrait. I'll pay you a thousand dollars to model for me tonight. I have a studio not too far from here."

*That woman must not have been lying about his wealth,* Heidi thought. "I'll tell you what," she said, withdrawing a pen and a pad from her purse. "Sketch my face right now. If I like what I see, I'll be your model for the night."

He quickly sketched her face, then returned the pen and the pad.

"Oh my god," Heidi said. "This is amazing."

"So you'll go with me?"

She looked into his eyes. "Absolutely."

He took a thousand dollars from his wallet and handed her the money. She put the money in her purse. They left.

***

Liam's car—a blue Bentley—was probably worth more money than Heidi had ever seen in her life. She didn't ask about his wealth, however. Or his family. Or his twin brother Alec that the woman in the club had mentioned.

Heidi figured that Liam would talk about those things if and when he wanted to.

They talked about art all the way to Liam's place, which was somewhere off the freeway just outside of Boston. They had to go up a private quarter-mile road to reach the house, which was large and beautiful and looked about a hundred years old.

"There's a barn around back," Liam said. "My studio's in the loft."

He drove around back to a massive barn behind the house. It was the largest barn Heidi had ever seen. Liam got out, opened a padlock, and pushed the barn door along its rails, making enough room to drive his car through. The interior of the barn was so black it swallowed his headlights. He got back in, drove forward, and then shut off the engine.

"It's so dark," Heidi said.

"Wait here."

Liam got out. He found the power box easily in the gloom. He pushed the switch upward. Rows of overhead cage lights flickered and then came on throughout the interior.

Heidi got out of the car. The barn was two stories tall. Stalls lined two walls on the first floor, and the top floor was a wraparound loft. She closed her eyes and breathed in deeply. The smell of horses reminded her of childhood back home in West Virginia. "This is nice."

"Come on," Liam said.

She followed him upstairs. He had a minibar in his studio.

Liam made her a drink. The fast-acting sedative he mixed in took effect soon thereafter and she passed out.

***

A shock of pain snapped her back to consciousness. No longer in the barn, Heidi stood naked and chained to a cinderblock wall in a room with no windows.

Liam stood before her, likewise naked. A blank canvas was mounted behind him. He held a scalpel in one hand and a paintbrush in the other.

Heidi said, "Why are you doing this to me?"

He smiled. "I'm going to paint your portrait. A series of them, actually."

He went to work on her with the scalpel. It went on for a very long time.

***

He found a teenage girl the following day and paid her to model for him, too. Then he fed her corpse to the pigs out back.

***

That night, Liam stood at the living-room window and watched the headlights of a car as it pulled up the long driveway. He flipped a switch by the door and four huge spotlights—mounted to the front of the house—came on and lit up the land beyond the window: the yard; the asphalt driveway; the massive trees that concealed his house from the road.

The car—a silver Mercedes that looked brand new—pulled to a stop in front of the house and the engine shut off. Liam didn't recognize the car, but it probably belonged to his twin brother Alec. His brother changed cars as often as some men changed razorblades.

Liam nevertheless grabbed a handgun off the coffee table. Then he heard a car door slam. He stepped outside and saw Alec standing beside the Mercedes. He approached his twin brother, and they embraced.

"It's good to see you, brother," Liam said.

"It's good to see you too, brother," Alec said. "You never answer your phone, so I was hoping I could find you here." He took an envelope from his jacket and handed it to Liam.

"What's this?" Liam said.

"The deed and the keys to a lighthouse."

"A lighthouse?"

"Yes. Our great-great-grandmother Virginia finally died. She was ninety-five. She left you the lighthouse in her will. She thought maybe you'd like to go there and paint seascapes from time to time."

Liam put the envelope in his jacket's interior pocket. "I don't remember exactly where that is."

"It's on a cliff overlooking Serenity Bay," Alec said. "About an hour north of here. We used to go play on Gull's Point when we were kids."

Liam nodded, and a smile formed on his face. "Ah, okay. I remember Gull's Point."

"And speaking of play," Alec said. "I brought something for us to play with tonight. It's in the trunk."

They walked to the back of the car, and Alec opened the trunk. Inside, a gagged and bound young woman looked up at them, terrified. She was bleeding from her nose and a cut above one eye.

"Nice," Liam said. "Let's take her down to the basement."

They did.

They stripped her naked and strapped her atop a steel operating table. There was a drain beneath the table in the center of the concrete floor.

The twins removed their clothes and put them on a long metal table by the door. There was a large surgical tray on the table. From the tray, Liam selected a scalpel and a retractor. Alec selected needle-nose pliers and a blowtorch.

"This will be fun," Alec said. "Just like the good old days."

Liam nodded. Then he reached behind him and closed the door.

***

Later, after they fed the woman's corpse to the pigs, Alec said, "I can stay here with the animals for a couple of days, if you want to go spend a night or two at your new lighthouse."

Liam packed a few things and headed north.

***

It was after four a.m. when Liam parked his car atop the cliff overlooking Serenity Bay. He wanted to stretch his legs, and decided to walk around the property. Leaving his suitcase on the passenger's seat, he shut the engine off and got out of the car.

The air was cool, but there was no wind. Visibility was excellent. The moon was full and there were no clouds in the sky.

The lighthouse was a cylindrical cast-iron tower that stood over a hundred feet tall. The keeper's quarters was a two-story brick house about three hundred feet from the lighthouse.

While walking a path along the cliff's edge, Liam's attention was attracted by what he at first thought might be a large fish stranded down on the shore, flapping around in distress. Or a wounded animal, perhaps, that glistened a pinkish-white in the moonlight. He stopped, wishing he had a pair of binoculars. An old ladder-type staircase had been constructed down the face of the high cliff not far from where he stood, and he hurried down the long steep ladder to the shore at the bottom of the cliff.

There was still quite a bit of distance and several weedy boulders between Liam and whatever it was, but it now seemed to be made up of eight or nine rounded body parts that were stuck together haphazardly. He thought it was strange, but he was not afraid. He pulled the loaded pistol from the waistband of his jeans and approached it.

As he drew closer, he saw that it was not one creature, but many. Their rounded bodies came apart when they caught sight of him, and the pinkish-white carcass on which they had been feeding was revealed to be the half-devoured body of a human being. Liam couldn't tell if the remains were of a male or a female. Each of the ghastly-looking creatures was shaped somewhat like an octopus, with long, thick, and flexible tentacles. They had large, intelligent-looking eyes that gave the grotesque suggestion of a face. Their bodies were about the size of the pigs he fed his victims to. Their tentacles were many feet in length.

And then a haunting, beautiful voice began to sing. A female's voice, sensual and fluid. Liam looked out at the jumble of rocks that made up Gull's Point—a stone promontory that jutted out into the ocean. He saw a naked woman sitting on a rock maybe a dozen yards away. She was sitting with her back to him, facing the sea. Her long wavy hair was a lustrous red in the moonlight.

At the sound of her voice, the nine or ten tentacled creatures—as one—abandoned the corpse on which they had been feasting and slithered out onto the promontory, toward the woman. To Liam's surprise, the creatures didn't stop when they reached her. He had been expecting them to gather around her like cobras mesmerized by a snake charmer's flute. Instead, as the woman continued to sing, all of the creatures slithered out into the sea and swam away.

Liam approached the woman. Her pitch-perfect voice seemed to warm his blood and chill it simultaneously.

The lyrics of the song she sang were in a language he didn't know, but he had never heard a more hypnotic melody in his life.

When Liam reached the woman, he sat down on the flat rock right beside her, facing the sea. He put a hand on her shoulder. Her flesh was cold. Still singing, she turned her head and looked at him with the brightest green eyes he had ever seen. The beauty of her face momentarily took his breath away. Then he lowered his hand and noticed that the texture of the woman's body changed beneath her waist. He looked down. She had the smooth skin of a woman all the way down to her upper thighs, but beneath those her body was covered in iridescent scales that glinted like silver-blue metal in the moonlight.

Still singing, she drew his face toward hers for a kiss. Her melody—as light and sweet as air—captured him with amber notes so pure they lured him in. By the time he surfaced from her musical spell and noticed that the song had ended, his throat burned as if it were on fire. He opened his mouth to speak, but gurgled on his own blood.

The woman smiled. His blood covered her mouth and dripped down her chest like red wax melting in the moonlight.

Then she savagely attacked his throat again with her claws and her teeth. The last thing he saw was his own decapitated body bleeding all over the rock as she raised his severed head and made him look at it.

***

Alec parked his car beside Liam's car atop the cliff overlooking Serenity Bay. He had not heard from his brother in four days. He had tried calling him several times, but of course Liam never answered his phone. And so he had driven an hour north to tell his brother that he was going to California for a couple of days.

Alec got out of the car. The night was mild. The moon was bright. He saw Liam's suitcase on the passenger's seat of his car, so maybe he was planning to leave soon.

He went to the keeper's quarters first and knocked on the door, but no one answered. He tried to open the door, but it was locked. Then he walked over to the lighthouse and found that it was locked up, too. *Perhaps Liam,* he thought, *has an easel set up around back and is working on a seascape.*

Alec went around back. While walking a path along the cliff's edge, he heard a woman's voice singing from below. Her voice was pitch-perfect. The melody she sang was the most beautiful piece of music he had ever heard. He walked to the cliff's edge and looked down. The voice belonged to a woman with red hair who was sitting on one of the rocks of the promontory, facing the ocean and singing in the moonlight.

Alec found an old ladder-type staircase and descended to the bottom of the cliff. The beauty of the music quickly drew him to the woman and the waves.

# CASA FIESTA

*You should not travel alone to Mexico.* She could still hear Dean's words ringing in her head. *Too many bad things can happen to a woman by herself down in Mexico.*

Karen usually went everywhere alone, and that was almost always by choice. Besides, she had already been to Mexico several times. She had never been *here* before, however, in the city of El Tajín, and she had always wanted to see the Pyramid of the Niches. But she wasn't going to make it to the pyramid today. She was tired, she needed a drink, and heavy rain forced her to search for a place to pull over.

She saw what looked like a restaurant or a hotel through sheets of rain pelting her windshield. She turned off onto a gravel drive that led to several empty parking spots near the main entrance. A man wearing a white jacket rushed out and opened an umbrella over her driver's-side door.

Karen got out. The waiter walked her into the restaurant and seated her at a table. Her Spanish was rusty, but the waiter spoke English. She ordered a glass of scotch with a few rocks of ice. After she drank it, she decided to rent a cabin behind the restaurant. The waiter was nice. He checked her in from her table and handed her a key.

Later, after a short nap, she went into the bar and ordered another glass of scotch. The bartender was nice, and he too spoke English. Karen took her drink to a table and sat down by herself.

She had broken up with Dean last week, walking away from yet another decent relationship. She loved him, and he loved her, but both of them knew it just wasn't right. He wanted kids, and she had never been the marrying type. She was happier sitting alone with strangers in a Mexican dive than she would ever be at any point during a marriage. Saddening, perhaps, but better than living a lie.

A good-looking man walked over to her table. Mexican. Maybe thirty. He was dressed nice and smelled like cologne. He smiled. His teeth were white. "Hello," he said. "Are you here alone?"

Karen nodded.

"Do you mind if I sit down?"

Karen took a drink. "Be my guest."

He sat down. "I'm Carlos."

"Nice to meet you, Carlos. I'm Karen."

"Are you American?"

"Yes. I'm from New York."

"Ah, yes. New York. Beautiful city. Are you here to see the pyramid?"

"Yes. I'm staying here tonight, and I'd like to ride by horseback to the pyramid tomorrow."

Carlos arched his eyebrows. "Where I work is the best place for horseback riding. Go to the Casa Fiesta Lodge tomorrow. Ask for either me or Antonio. One of us will take you to the pyramid."

Karen finished her drink. "Thank you, Carlos. Maybe I'll see you tomorrow." She stood up.

"There's another bar close to here," Carlos said, "that is more relaxing."

She looked into his eyes. “No thank you, Carlos. It’s been a long day, and I need to get some sleep.”

“Don’t forget,” he said. “Casa Fiesta Lodge. It’s not far from here. You’ll see the sign on your way to the pyramid.”

Karen smiled and nodded. Then she walked away.

***

The next day was sunny. Karen found the sign for the Casa Fiesta Lodge along a cutback in the road. She turned onto a gravel drive and went up a steep hill. The lodge became visible from the top. At the bottom, she parked and got out. There was only one other vehicle in front, an SUV with a rental-car sticker on the bumper.

She went in. The interior was dark and quiet. She didn’t see anyone inside. She made her way around a couple of wooden tables and then leaned against the kitchen counter. She could smell something cooking. “Hello!” she called into the darkness.

She heard someone moving around back there. She also heard what sounded like pots and pans banging against each other. Then a tall thin Mexican male stepped into view. “Are you Antonio?” Karen said.

He smiled. “Yes. Welcome to the Casa Fiesta Lodge.”

"I'm Karen. Carlos sent me. He told me you could help me. I want to go to the pyramid on horseback."

"Ah. So you want to ride the trails?"

"Yes."

"Excellent." He smiled again. "Have a seat. I'll be ready soon." He walked away.

Karen sat down.

Antonio returned moments later holding a machete.

"Nice knife," Karen said.

"To clear the trail," he said. "Come on. Let's go."

She followed him outside.

Two horses were saddled up around back. One was brown; the other was black. Antonio patted the black horse. "This one is yours," he said. "Diablo." He mounted the brown horse and holstered the machete in his saddle. Karen mounted Diablo.

"Do you have friends with you in Mexico?" Antonio said.

"No," Karen said. "I'm here alone."

He led her up the road she drove in on, then turned onto a path of dirt and rock. The trail got worse as they advanced. The slopes were muddy and uneven. After a while they turned off the path onto a narrow trail and began a steep climb through the forest. Antonio pulled out his machete and hacked at the shrubs and brush. They followed the trail up several switchbacks and repeatedly crossed over a stream.

They emerged from the forest eventually into an open meadow. The lodge was visible below. Karen took a photo of a small waterfall. They continued up the hill, entered more forest, and then another clearing appeared. They crossed the clearing and ascended to the crest. They dismounted their horses at the top.

The pyramid was visible, but still a long distance away; it was far below on the other side of a wide valley. Karen said, "What the hell is this?"

She was just about to turn around when agony exploded through her body. She looked down at her chest and saw the end of the machete sticking out of it. There was more agony as Antonio ripped the machete out of her. Then her shirt started soaking up a whole lot of blood.

Antonio grabbed her scalp by the roots of her hair and spun her around. He held the machete high with hatred blazing in his eyes. Then he swung the machete at her neck.

Karen's last sight was that of her bleeding, decapitated body hitting the ground. Then blackness.

***

Antonio spread the body out on the ground and stripped the clothes away. He pressed the machete's tip into each of the major joints, separating the cartilage. Then he raised the blade and chopped down on those places to cut through cartilage and ligaments. Soon he had the arm pieces, the leg pieces, the torso, and the head all separated.

He grabbed a sharp knife from a saddle holster. He held the thigh of a leg at an angle against a rock. He sliced the meat from the bone in large fillets. He put the meat in one black trash bag and the bones in another. He repeated the process for each of the limb parts and then the torso. He put the heart, kidneys, and liver in the meat bag. He put the head in the meat bag, too.

He double-bagged each trash bag and draped them over Diablo's saddle, tying the knotted parts around the saddle horn. He put the woman's backpack, clothes, and shoes in a third bag and draped it over Diablo's saddle, too.

Antonio stopped on the way back down and washed his hands, machete, and knife in the waterfall. Then he and the two horses resumed their journey back down the mountain.

***

"Your husband melted?" the Mexican male said.

Sandra nodded. "Yes. On his twenty-sixth birthday. Michael was older than me. I'm still twenty-three."

"How did it happen?"

"Michael worked at a steel mill."

"In America?"

"Yes. Pennsylvania."

"Is that close to New York?"

"No. Same time zone, but not exactly close." Sandra sipped her drink. "Anyway, Michael was operating the remote control of a ladle belt. The ladle belt was a conveyor suspended high above the floor. It transferred large tubs of molten steel from the melting furnace to the holding furnace. There was an explosion. High above where Michael was standing, one of the tubs tipped over and dumped five hundred tons of molten steel directly onto his head."

"Hostia puta!"

Sandra sipped her drink. "Once the spill cooled and workers were able to get to him, what remained was more a block of steel than a human being."

"That's terrible."

"Yes. But at least he died instantly. The coroner told me later that Michael probably never felt a thing."

"Was there a lawsuit? A settlement?"

"Yes," Sandra said. "I received a fairly large sum of money. Michael and I had a bucket list, and going horseback riding in Egypt to see the pyramids was on the list. That's why I'm here. I thought it was too dangerous to go overseas to Egypt, so I decided to come to Mexico instead. What's your name again?"

"Carlos."

Sandra wrote it down. "And you can take me to see the pyramid on horseback in the morning?"

"Yes. Go to the Casa Fiesta Lodge. It's not far from here. You'll see the sign on your way to the pyramid. When you get there, ask for either me or Antonio."

Sandra wrote down the information. Then she finished her drink and stood up. "Thank you, Carlos. I'll see you tomorrow."

He smiled. "I look forward to it."

## LONG WAY HOME

Mya returned to her childhood home and found it had not changed one bit. The house looked the same as it always did. When she saw her parents standing in the doorway waiting to welcome her in, she knew she would be unable to pretend that nothing had happened. Soon she would have to tell them the terrible news.

Her father smiled. “You look great, Mya. It’s good to see you again. Come on in.”

Her mother took her carry-on. “You’ll have to stay in the guest room tonight. Is that okay?”

Mya nodded. “Of course.” Her father loved antique model train sets and he probably had one set up in her old room right now.

Dinner was great. As always, her parents laughed and talked about a little bit of everything. Mya wanted to tell them both the terrible news right then and there, but she couldn’t do it. They looked so happy, and she didn’t want to ruin their happiness. Not yet, anyway. Maybe tomorrow. She knew that after she told them the news, nothing would ever be the same.

***

Mya woke up that night needing to use the bathroom. She made her way to the bathroom in the dark. While returning to the guest room, she saw the figure of a woman in the dark hallway who had to be her sister. Mya and Christina had always looked a lot alike.

Christina went into Mya's old bedroom and closed the door. Mya went to the door and knocked lightly. Christina didn't answer.

Mya tried to open the door, but it was locked. The door had a keyhole, but Mya didn't have a key. She had never needed to unlock the door from outside the room back when she still lived inside the house.

Mya returned to the guest room and went to bed. She didn't know if Christina had just now arrived, or if she had arrived a little earlier after Mya had fallen asleep. She was probably sleeping in a sleeping bag on the floor beside her father's train set. And she was probably listening to music with headphones on and hadn't heard Mya lightly knocking on the door.

And she was undoubtedly there for the same reason that Mya was there: to tell their beautiful parents the terrible news.

***

The next morning, the door to Mya's old bedroom was still locked. Mya had been hoping that her sister was already awake and had told their parents the news, but apparently she would have to be the one to do it.

She went downstairs. Her parents were seated on the living-room sofa, drinking coffee.

Her father smiled. "Good morning, dear. Want some coffee?"

Mya shook her head. "No thanks. Has Christina been downstairs yet this morning?"

"Christina?" her mother said. "Of course not, dear. Christina isn't here."

"That's odd," Mya said. "I thought I saw her last night. It must have been a dream. Anyway, there's something I need to tell you, but I think it would be easier just to show you." From behind her back Mya produced a section of a week-old newspaper. She opened it on the coffee table and pointed to what she wanted them to see.

Both leaned over and looked at the newspaper.

Her father shrugged. "Well, I suppose it *is* true, after all." He smiled at Mya, but his smile looked so sad.

"You knew?" Mya said.

"We suspected," her mother said. "But then we just simply brushed it aside. We thought that maybe it had all been a dream. That we were still . . ."

Again they looked down at their obituaries.

"We were on our way to see your sister," her father said, "when the plane went down."

"I know," Mya said. "Half the flight survived, and the other half did not. I think I will have a cup of coffee now."

She went into the kitchen and poured a cup of coffee. Then she went back into the living room.

Her parents were gone. Their coffee cups were dry. A key lay on the coffee table next to her mother's cup.

She picked up the key—and heard the sound of footsteps coming from her old room upstairs. Wondering who now occupied the room, Mya turned and headed up the stairs.

## LOSSES AND GAINS

Seeing her own reflection in the mirror behind the bar, Alicia wondered how any man could resist her. At twenty-seven, she knew she was more beautiful than the homecoming queen she had been at seventeen. She also knew that her beauty contributed to the small fortune she made in tips bartending at Shy-Anne's Saloon. Most nights, after the club closed, she left with any man of her choosing.

Occasionally, however, she actually *did* meet a man who could resist her, and she always seethed at the rejection.

Tonight she encountered one of those creatures.

***

She first became aware of the man sometime after midnight. He sat alone at the far end of the bar. Mid-twenties, probably. Possibly thirty. Dark eyes. Dark hair. Good-looking, certainly—but nothing spectacular. For some reason, though, Alicia found him irresistible, and she was puzzled by the strength of the attraction she felt for him. Inexplicably, she had to fight an urge to reach inside her pants and pleasure herself right there behind the bar. Curiously, the man wouldn't even look at her. He had not even acknowledged her existence.

Alicia mixed him a bourbon-and-soda. Then she set it down in front of him on the bar. “This one’s on me.” She gave him a wink.

The man smiled and raised the glass. “Thanks.”

In his eyes, Alicia saw no evidence of sexual interest. She felt the first stirrings of fury, but remained calm by telling herself that maybe the man was just shy. She extended a hand across the bar. “I’m Alicia.”

“Joshua.”

He shook her hand, and at the exact moment their fingers made contact, she twitched at the depth of the desire she felt for him immediately.

“I want to take you home,” Alicia said.

He shook his head. “I don’t think so.”

Alicia maintained her grin, but the fire within became an inferno. She was unaccustomed to such blatant rejection.

“I appreciate the drink,” Joshua said. “And you’re very beautiful. But I’m just not interested.”

Seething, Alicia nodded. “Okay.”

“It’s not you,” Joshua said. “It’s me. But I *would* still like to be your friend.”

Alicia said, “You want to be my friend?”

“Yes. I would like that.”

"Then come over to my place, after the club closes. We'll listen to music."

Joshua smiled. "It's a date."

***

Alicia's house wasn't far from Shy-Anne's Saloon, and Joshua followed her there in his car. Once inside, Alicia said, "The stereo's in my bedroom. Come on. Let's go listen to music."

He shot her a funny look.

"Don't worry," she said. "The minibar's in there, too. I promise I won't try to seduce you."

Joshua smiled. "I'm not worried."

She led him into her room. "Have a seat."

He sat down on her bed. Alicia made him a drink. Then she jammed a hypodermic needle into his neck, pressed the plunger, and Joshua passed out.

She gagged him. She removed his shoes, jacket, and clothes. His penis was impressive even though it was flaccid, and she suspected that it was massive when erect. She stripped her bed and covered the mattress with a plastic painter's tarp. She had to move his body around to get all of the tarp beneath him, but it wasn't too difficult. Then she rolled him onto his back and handcuffed his wrists and ankles to the four posts of the bed.

She opened a bottle of ammonia beneath his nose and woke him up.

Joshua's eyes—to Alicia's pleasant surprise—appeared to be clear, alert, and not at all confused from any lingering effects of the sedative. She gave him some time to take in his predicament. He swept his gaze around the room, and surprised her again by not attempting to mumble into his gag.

"I don't have any close neighbors," Alicia said. "And even if I did, it wouldn't matter. See all these tiles on the walls and the ceiling? Soundproof insulation. Acoustic foam."

She held up a power drill and revved it. Joshua's eyes widened.

"We're going to listen to some music, all right," Alicia said. "We're going to listen to the music of your screams all night long."

Joshua tugged at the handcuffs. Chains rattled. Alicia thought she detected a flash of panic in his eyes, but then he surprised her again: he started laughing.

She cocked her head. "You think it's funny?" She lowered the power drill and grabbed his scrotum. She singled out one of his testicles and pushed the point of the drill bit against it. "Then you'll definitely get a kick out of this." She pressed the trigger. The drill bit went all the way through his testicle. Blood flowed copiously. Joshua writhed in pain. His screams through the gag were music to her ears.

Alicia put the power drill down. She couldn't believe how wet she was. "Don't go anywhere. I'll be right back."

She left the bed and returned moments later with a big glass dildo. She pleasured herself to a climax. Then she pulled some pliers and a carving knife out of her nightstand. She positioned the jaws of the pliers around one of his nipples and lightly clamped the tips. Joshua looked at her. Alicia squeezed the handles. Joshua smiled around the gag in his mouth. Furious, Alicia increased the pressure. Joshua's eyes bulged and he issued a deep guttural whine. Alicia smiled.

Then she cut his nipple off with the carving knife. Joshua shrieked. Alicia put the nipple in her mouth and ate it.

She did the same thing to his other nipple. Then she fucked herself again with the dildo, quickly reaching another climax.

To stem the twin streams of blood running down Joshua's chest, Alicia cauterized the wounds with a blowtorch. The smell of burning flesh filled the air. Fire blackened his skin and created new nipples of char where the old nipples had been cut away.

Then she moved the blowtorch over Joshua's torso, letting him feel the heat, but not letting the fire touch his flesh. The skin reddened. Blisters formed and burst, oozing clear liquids that the blowtorch quickly boiled away.

Joshua's eyes rolled back in his head and he lost consciousness. Alicia woke him up with the ammonia and started fucking herself again. She didn't know that the glass phallus had somehow broken inside her until she looked down and noticed that she was bleeding. She exchanged the broken phallus for a bigger plastic dildo and pleasured herself to a third shrieking orgasm.

She removed Joshua's gag. "Anything you want to say now, pretty boy?"

He smiled and didn't say anything.

She went to work on his face with a straight razor. She sliced one of his ears off and ate it. She sawed his nose off and tossed it aside. She cut his lips off and ate both of those. She extracted four of his upper teeth with the pliers and dropped them into a bedside trashcan.

Joshua made a lot of noise, but he never said a word.

"I don't get it," Alicia said. "You weren't *all* that good-looking to begin with. Handsome, yes, but not *exceptionally*. And now you're absolutely hideous. So why in the hell am I still attracted to you?"

He laughed. Blood poured from his mouth. Alicia scorched his penis with the blowtorch and he screamed.

She fucked herself again, and noticed that she was now bleeding profusely when she climaxed.

She started peeling away layers of flesh from his abdomen with the straight razor. He passed out. She splashed rubbing alcohol over his wounds and woke him up.

Alicia searched his eyes, and did not find what she expected. There was agony, to be sure, but she saw no shock or sense of disbelief. His eyes seemed to mock her. Something about Joshua just wasn't right.

She attacked his genitals with the blowtorch, burning away his scrotum and his testicles, not stopping until he was a eunuch. He screamed a lot throughout the castration, but Joshua never lost consciousness. For good measure, Alicia went ahead and burned away his penis.

Then she had to fuck herself again. She knew that she was losing a lot of blood, but she couldn't stop herself. Despite feeling lightheaded, her sex drive was insatiable.

When she came, her urethra burned like she had an infection.

But still she couldn't stop.

By dawn, she had climaxed ten more times, each orgasm more painful than the last. She thought about burning away or cutting off her fingers, but she finally managed to gain control of her hands. To her horror, however, she discovered that she no longer needed to touch herself to climax. Her body became wracked with orgasms beyond her control. Time and again a searing pain bloomed deep inside her and sent blood shooting out of her vagina. She screamed every time, and frequently burst into tears, fearing that each orgasm would kill her.

By noon, Joshua barely looked human anymore. His entire body was shredded and scorched. He was still alive, though. He watched Alicia's every move with eyes that seemed hyperaware of everything.

Sometime around midnight, Alicia found herself clutching a bedpost with one hand to keep herself upright while her other hand swiped listlessly at Joshua with the straight razor. A final, agonizing orgasm exploded throughout her body. And then she died.

The bedroom was silent, but not for long.

Soon thereafter, chains rattled and Joshua cleared his throat. "Was that as good for you as it was for me?"

He looked down with new eyes that were green instead of brown at new skin that was clean and unblemished. Then he easily broke away from the handcuffs and rose from the bed.

He dressed in the same clothes that his old body had been wearing when he got there. And then he left.

## DELIVERANCE

Lightning cracked, thunder roared, and cold rain poured from a storm-blackened sky. Ron Meadows sat on an old steel chair on his front porch and watched ankle-deep mudholes form in his front yard. At one time, his yard had been pretty, and he had taken pride in it, mowing at least once a week. Flowers used to bloom in the flowerbeds.

Now his front yard was nothing but dirt in dry weather and mud when wet. He no longer used his garage, and that was for the sole purpose of driving and parking in the yard, killing all of the grass.

He didn't want a pretty yard. He wanted a dirty, dusty landscape. He didn't want flowers in the flowerbeds, for he no longer found any beauty in nature whatsoever.

Where some people may find pleasure when viewing a flower, he found only bittersweet memories of Molly and Stacie. Because the bitter outweighed the sweet, he had uprooted every flower in his yard, not only killing them, but ripping each flower to shreds.

He had taken no pleasure in the destruction of the flowers; to his surprise, he had cried throughout the entire process. But the choice between having a pretty yard without Molly and Stacie alive to see it, or a barren yard of dirt and mud to coexist with his loneliness—to him—was no choice at all.

The storm raged on, and the wind's speed increased. He took a drink of whiskey, screwed the cap back on the bottle, and stood up.

The clanging wind chimes, to Ron, sounded like a language of the damned. He tore them down from the roof of the porch and tossed them into the mud. The wind chimes were stilled, but the storm sounded like laughter. Cursing, he walked into his house.

In the house, no pictures of Molly or Stacie adorned the walls or the tables. Their images were burned into his memory, and he needed no reminders of their beauty. His tears flowed freely enough, and when gazing upon pictures of his dead wife and daughter, the longing to be reunited with his family made him want to kill himself.

But he resisted suicide. He considered suicide a sin. As angry at God as he was, he also *feared* God. Any god that would take a man's wife and daughter from him would surely condemn his soul to damnation. Though suicide was not an option, Ron still wanted to die.

He sat down on his couch—and was about to take another drink of whiskey when the telephone rang. *Strange.* Who on Earth would be calling him? He had no family or friends.

The old landline telephone sat on an end table next to the couch, allowing him to answer without getting up. "Hello?"

"Hello, Ron."

It was Maria—Molly's mother, and Stacie's grandmother. Her voice had always soothed him, but today she sounded sad.

"Hi, Maria."

"Listen, Ron, I just got to worrying about you, and figured I'd call and see how you were doing."

"I'm doing okay, I guess. How are you?"

"I'm all right, I suppose. I'm sorry I haven't called you sooner, but whenever I think about it . . . well . . . I just start crying."

Maria was religious. Her belief that her daughter's and her granddaughter's souls were in God's eternal kingdom of Heaven was strong. Nevertheless, their deaths had shaken her Christian faith to her core.

"I know, Maria. It's just so hard to find joy in anything anymore. Their absence is killing me slowly. I honestly wish I were dead."

"Me too, Ron. They were all that I had, too."

"I know."

After a moment of silence, Ron shared a spontaneous idea. "I'm thinking of going to Boulder," he said.

*"Boulder?* Why?"

"I don't know. I've never been there, for one thing. And it's where they died, for another thing."

"I still don't understand why you'd want to go there."

"Neither do I." He really didn't. The decision to drive to Colorado had come from out of nowhere.

"Then why go?"

"I don't know. Maybe I'll feel a sense of closure, or something."

"When are you going?"

"Right now."

*"Right now?"*

"Yes."

"Why right now?"

"Why *not* right now? I'm not doing anything. I haven't worked for months. I've barely been out of the house at all. I'm leaving today. I think I'll drive."

"That's quite a drive, Ron."

"About a thousand miles. Maybe sixteen, seventeen hours. It might do me some good."

"Well, you be careful out there."

"I will. Take care of yourself, Maria."

"You too, Ron. Goodbye."

"Goodbye."

Ron hung up the phone. He got up from the couch and took a shot of whiskey.

He needed a few things. *Money?* He checked his wallet: about two hundred in cash and the gold card. *Clothes?* He went into his bedroom, grabbed a duffel bag from the closet, and put some clean clothes in it. Then he took a toothbrush, toothpaste, comb, and deodorant from the bathroom and put those in the duffel bag, too.

He went into the kitchen, grabbed his car keys, and was headed toward the door when a word popped into his head: *gun*. Gun? *Where in the hell had that come from?* He didn't need a gun. But then again, he didn't need to drive over a thousand miles just to see the piece of Earth where Molly and Stacie died. The decision to visit Boulder had popped into his head as suddenly and unexpectedly as the word *gun*.

He went back into the bedroom, opened a drawer in the nightstand, and withdrew his .45 automatic. He tossed the Glock into his duffel bag, along with the two boxes of ammunition that he kept in the drawer.

He left.

In his car, he put the keys in the ignition, but paused before starting the engine. "Ron Meadows," he said. "What the fuck are you doing?"

He started the engine and drove away.

***

During the drive, Ron entertained himself with sweet memories of good times shared with Molly and Stacie. He remembered the time they included Stacie—then five—with his and Molly's seventh wedding anniversary by taking a family trip to Disneyland, and how Stacie's eyes had glowed with such wonder in the magical world of Mickey and crew.

She had been such a beautiful child. After they entered Stacie in her first beauty pageant, they were not surprised when she won. Molly had been gorgeous, with glorious blonde hair and brown eyes. Stacie had blonde hair like Molly's, but she got her blue eyes from Ron: blue eyes as clear as the waters of a lagoon, with an inner light that to him was all but blinding.

He recalled how animals were naturally drawn to Stacie—and not just dogs and cats, either. One summer day, when Stacie was six years old, Ron had taught her to fly a kite. During the experience, a sparrow descended from the clear blue skies and landed on her shoulder. He had been stunned by the wonder and mystery of the moment, but Stacie hadn't made a big deal of it. She had simply said, "Look, Daddy. It likes me."

***

The miles to Boulder lessened, and so too did the car's fuel supply. Ron spotted a sign indicating that gas and food were available at the next exit. He left the interstate, took a right, and pulled into a gas station's parking lot.

He paid for the gas at the pump, then went inside to get snacks for the road.

While browsing a rack of potato chips and candy bars, another word popped into his head: *paper*. Paper? What the hell was that supposed to mean? The word repeated over and over in his head: *paper, paper, paper, paper*. He couldn't stop it. It felt as if someone else were saying it to him, but only in his mind—telepathically.

He wondered if he might be losing his mind.

*Paper, paper, paper.*

"Newspaper, perhaps?" he whispered.

*No! Paper, paper, paper.*

He skipped selecting a snack and approached the cash register.

The cashier—a young man of nineteen or twenty, perhaps—smiled at him. "How are you doing today, sir?"

"Just fine. How about you?"

"Just fine, thanks. Anything else you need, besides the gas?"

*Paper! Paper! Paper!*

Ron said, "Do you have any paper?"

"Paper? You mean like acid? LSD?"

"No. A sheet of paper."

"Oh. Okay. Let me check."

The cashier searched beneath the register and found a notebook. He flipped through it to a blank page, tore it out, and handed it to Ron. "Will one page be enough?"

"Yes. Thanks."

"No problem."

Ron turned to leave, and once again a word popped into his head: *pencil*. He left the store and headed toward his car with the word *pencil* being repeated in his mind.

"There's a pen in the car," Ron whispered.

It stopped. Just like that.

He opened the driver's-side door and got in. He opened the glove compartment, found an ink pen, and took it out. Holding the pen in front of his face, he studied it as if it were an ancient artifact.

What in the world had gotten into him? First, the spur-of-the-moment decision to drive to Boulder. Then, a desire to bring a gun. No, that wasn't right, actually. The word *gun* had simply popped into his head. And now more words were popping into his mind for no reason, as if someone or something were putting them there.

But that was crazy, right? Nobody was sending him telepathic messages, were they? No, of course not. He had heard of people going insane from grief. Could that be what was happening to him? Did he miss his wife and daughter so much that his brain had stopped functioning properly? It was a question he could not answer. He didn't feel crazy, but knew he was acting it.

And pencil? Seriously? He couldn't remember the last time he had written anything with a pencil. He preferred a pen. If he *were* subconsciously sending the messages to himself, he would have used the word pen, not pencil. It didn't make any sense.

From the glove compartment, he withdrew the owner's manual and placed the sheet of paper on top of it, in case he inexplicably decided to write something.

That's when he lost control of his hands. His right hand wrote the letter *S*. He tried to stop writing, and succeeded—but with difficulty. It were as if an external force wanted to write something for him, using his hand. Again, he questioned his sanity.

"Fuck it," Ron said. "If you want to write something, then write."

He stopped resisting the pull of the invisible force, and went with it.

His hand spelled two words: *STACIE. ALIVE.*

He sat staring at those two words for what seemed at least two minutes. All capital letters, and the penmanship was definitely not his own. The words appeared to be composed in a child's chaotic scrawl. He remembered so much about Stacie, but not what her handwriting had looked like.

The possibilities were few. One: he was insane. He had heard that only an insane person would never question their sanity, but he didn't believe he was losing his mind. Two: someone with psychic abilities was playing a cruel joke on him. But who? He had no enemies, and he certainly had no psychic foes that he was aware of. No, he didn't buy that theory, either.

His hand began to write again: *ME DADDY. ALIVE.*

Could it be? Could Stacie possibly be alive? After all, he had not seen her body—or Molly's either, for that matter. Molly's car had flipped, rolled, and exploded into a burning pile of metal. The authorities had told him there were no bodies to identify, that there were scarcely any remains at all.

Could Stacie have somehow survived, and staggered away from the wreckage before anyone found it?

But that didn't explain the psychic aspect of the situation. How had she developed the telepathic abilities to send messages to his mind? And how had she developed the telekinetic abilities to move his hand from whatever distance separated them?

Ron started the car and resumed his journey to Boulder. He believed he would find his answers there.

***

He studied her closely.

The girl hadn't responded to physical torture for over a month and a half. She was an extremely tough little bitch. He missed hearing her exquisite screams during their sessions. It just wasn't the same without her twitching and thrashing. She used to struggle so furiously, turning her face away from his various instruments of torture.

She could still feel pain, though. He was sure of it. She had simply learned, somehow, to diminish his pleasure by not responding.

***

Ron's anxiety increased the closer he got to Boulder. He could feel Stacie's presence; he was sure of that. He no longer questioned his sanity, but he questioned everything else.

He had never been to Colorado in his life. Before he lost Molly and Stacie, he had owned a successful construction company in Houston, Texas. It was a fast-paced line of work, and he liked to be in town to oversee all of his projects.

When Stacie won the Little Miss Texas beauty pageant, she became a national contender. The nationals were held in Boulder, Colorado. The categories and events of the national finals lasted the duration of one week. Ron couldn't leave Houston for a week, so Molly and Stacie had gone without him. They took a first-class flight to Boulder, and Molly had rented a car in advance.

According to the authorities, Molly had lost control of her vehicle during their fourth day in Boulder. It had flipped, rolled, and exploded. There had been no remains of Molly or Stacie worth viewing.

However, Stacie was somewhere. Somehow, she had survived the wreck. And if she was still alive, what about Molly? Could his wife still possibly be alive?

Ron was simultaneously filled with hope and dread.

Straight ahead, a big green sign read BOULDER NEXT 4 EXITS.

***

He was a very spiritual man. There was no doubt in his mind that consciousness survived death. The problem was that he had never heard of a religion that coincided with his beliefs. His philosophy was that life was all about pain. The more pain a person received in this life, the greater their rewards in the next. And the more pain a person administered in this life, the greater their chances of being a god in the afterlife—not merely receiving awards, but bestowing them.

He was so confident in his future godhood that he almost couldn't wait to die.

And every day he prayed thanks to the dark gods who had provided him with Molly and Stacie Meadows.

It had been an ordinary day. He had been driving around, routinely patrolling a neighborhood. On a quiet street, he had seen an overturned car in the distance. As he drove closer, he saw a very attractive woman and the most beautiful little girl he had ever seen. The woman—presumably the mother—waved to him for help.

He stopped. He gave them a ride, all right, but not before reading them their rights and handcuffing them. Then he put them in the back of his squad car.

The woman's overturned car was the result of a blown tire. Her car's explosion was the result of a few lit matches and a bullet fired into its fuel tank.

There had been no witnesses around to see the abduction.

The girl—Stacie—had been dressed in a beautiful gown. He had later learned that she was in town for a beauty pageant.

He would never forget that first night with them, alone, in his basement.

Molly, the mother, had tried so hard to convince him to let the little girl go. He could smell the desperation in her tears, and he could hear it in her delirious motherly pleas.

He had known that those two would be fun, and was anxious to see which one of them went insane first.

As it turned out, the mother hadn't lasted nearly as long as her daughter. After seeing her daughter's teeth knocked out with a hammer, and one eye plucked out with a straight-head screwdriver, her grip on sanity had rapidly loosened.

Eventually—after she screamed, writhed, thrashed, laughed, and did everything else that people do when driven insane—she chewed off her own tongue and choked on it. He found her the next morning, blue with bulging eyes. For his own amusement, he forced Stacie to stare at her decomposing mother for two weeks. When the stench became too nauseating even for him, he found other ways to amuse himself through the physical and psychological torture of Stacie.

But something in her had changed. She was alive, barely, but she no longer responded to physical torture. It wasn't as fun for him as it used to be.

He approached Stacie, who lay strapped—flat on her back—to a wooden rack.

"I know you can hear me, princess."

She didn't reply.

He grabbed an icepick from his instrument table. He slammed it into her stomach, deep, all the way to the handle.

She didn't even flinch. Yet still she continued to breathe, even though there wasn't much left of her physical form.

He prayed and asked the dark gods he loved to repair her damaged nerve endings.

***

As Ron entered Boulder, Stacie began throwing words into his head relentlessly: *Alive. Slazzer. Paper. Alive.*

He had to pull over. He held the pen in one hand and the paper on the owner's manual across his lap.

Stacie wrote: *ALIVE, DADDY. I'M ALIVE.*

Ron began to cry. No other words could have made him any happier than those. Stacie was alive, she was in Boulder, and he was going to find her.

"Stacie, can you hear me?"

*Yes.*

She had not written the word. Perhaps her telepathic powers had increased as the distance between them had decreased. "Do I need the pen and paper anymore?"

*No.*

The word popped right into his head. He put the paper, the pen, and the owner's manual in the glove compartment and closed it.

"Stacie, where are you?"

*Slazzers.*

Slazzers. He didn't understand.

"Where's your mother?"

*Heaven.*

"She died in the explosion?"

*No. In Slazzers.*

Was Slazzer a place or a name?

"Stacie, what is Slazzer?"

*A very bad man. A terrible man.*

"Are you at Slazzer's house?"

*Yes. In his basement.*

"Do you know where he lives?"

*No Daddy. I love you.*

"I love you too, Stacie. I'm going to find you."

He retrieved his phone and called INFORMATION.

"Information. What city and state, please?"

"Boulder, Colorado."

"One moment please. Thank you for holding. What listing, please?"

"Slazzer."

"One moment, please."

After a few seconds of silence, the operator said, "Is that S-l-a-z-z-e-r?"

"Yes."

"We have no listing for anyone by that name, sir."

Ron terminated the call, frustrated, and confused. Stacie was somewhere in Boulder, but where?

*Straight.*

The word had suddenly popped into his head. Stacie had said that she didn't know where Slazzer lived, but perhaps she could simply sense her father's proximity and was somehow drawing him to her location. It was a wild theory, but he had nothing else to go on.

*Straight.*

The word popped into his head again. Stacie had sent it. He started the engine, put the car back on the road, and went straight.

"Is this the way, Stacie?"

She didn't telepathically answer. Perhaps she was saving her psychic energy for when she needed it most. He continued driving straight. Maybe five miles later, Stacie spoke: *Left*.

Straight ahead stood a 4-way stop sign at an intersection. He slowed to a stop at the sign and turned left, knowing in his heart that he was going the right way.

"I'm coming, Stacie. Just hold on. I'm coming."

Ron drove, weeping tears of joy, smiling while anticipating a miraculous reunion with his daughter.

***

He had an idea. If the little bitch was actually strong enough to block out the pain of physical torture, she was no doubt gaining strength by the minute.

He had one last option.

If he could burn one more scream out of her, he would be pleased. He decided to set what was left of her on fire.

He ascended the basement stairs, crossed the kitchen, and walked outside to his shed to get some gasoline.

***

Ron had been driving for several miles, beginning to get discouraged, when Stacie spoke again: *Left.*

He took a left onto a dirt road and went up a hill, at the top of which stood a one-story house. Parked in the driveway was a police car. The mailbox read SLAZZER.

*Yes, Daddy! This is it! Bring the gun! And be careful!*

Those were the first full sentences she had telepathically formed in his mind, as if the distance between them had limited her psychic abilities.

*Hurry, Daddy! He's going to burn me!*

Ron grabbed his gun, got out of the car, and rushed the house. He didn't bother knocking. He simply kicked in the door.

***

Slazzer was in the basement, about to douse Stacie with gasoline, when he heard the noise upstairs. First, the front door was kicked in. That was followed by footsteps, and then a man shouted one word: "Stacie!"

How in the hell could anyone know about Stacie? It was impossible. As far as anyone knew, she had been legally dead for over a year.

He heard the basement door open.

He grabbed his gun and retreated to a dark corner, giving himself the advantages of concealment and surprise, and watched a man rush down the stairs.

It was Ron Meadows. He recognized him from his year-old newspaper photos. Impossible! How could Stacie's father have even known she was alive? And how could he have possibly known she was here?

Emerging from the shadows, Slazzer cocked his gun.

***

When Ron reached the bottom of the stairs, he found Stacie—or what was left of her. She had been blinded and tortured beyond belief. Both of her eyes were missing, along with her tongue, teeth, nose, and ears. Her beautiful blonde hair had been pulled out; she was bald. Her arms were chopped off at the shoulders, and her legs were missing, as well. She lay on her back secured to a wooden rack by a leather strap across her chest.

Ron had not been expecting this.

He began to weep.

"It's okay Stacie. I'm here now. We're getting out of here."

Lightning cracked, thunder roared, and a storm broke in Boulder, Colorado.

"You're not going anywhere, Mr. Meadows."

Ron turned and stood face to face with his daughter's destroyer.

"Why?" Ron asked. "For the love of God, why have you done this to her?"

"You'd never understand," Slazzer replied. He then attempted to fire his gun at Ron's chest, but nothing happened. He tried to fire again—and again, nothing happened.

Ron—suspecting that Stacie was telekinetically keeping the trigger from being squeezed—raised his own gun, fired once, and saw Slazzer's head explode.

Then he approached Stacie, unstrapped her, lifted her from the wooden rack, and held her ruined torso in his arms. He cried despite trying desperately not to.

*Thanks, Daddy.*

He heard her words as clearly as if she had spoken them, but she was clearly incapable of speech—or anything else.

He remembered the sparrow landing on her shoulder.

To escape the torture, she had shut down her senses. After she accomplished sensory shutdown, her psychic abilities had grown stronger. That's how she had drawn him from Texas to Colorado.

She didn't explain this to him, nor did she have to. He simply knew.

*Take me outside, Daddy. Please.*

Ron carried her upstairs, across the kitchen, and outside into the merciless storm.

*Now shoot me.*

"Stacie, honey, I can't. I mean . . . we can try to—"

*No, Daddy. It's too late. Just shoot me.*

He thought about the first word that had popped into his mind in Houston: gun. Stacie had wanted him to bring the gun so that he could kill her and end her pain. That was why she had brought him here—so that he could deliver her from suffering.

And now she could deliver him from suffering, as well.

*I love you, Daddy.*

"I love you too, Stacie. Forever."

Ron shot her in the head, put the barrel in his mouth, and pulled the trigger.

The storm raged on without them, but for Ron and for Stacie, the mad laughter of the wind was stilled.

## HOLLYWOOD ENDING

"Thanks for auditioning," the casting director said. "You're a fine actor. I'll call you if you're chosen for the role."

Octavio handed her back the script. "Thanks for auditioning me."

He left.

The day was sunny, warm, and it was a Saturday. He didn't have to be back at work until Monday morning. He checked his phone to see what time it was: 11:11 a.m.

*Make a wish!* He wished that Verna took him more seriously as a love interest, that she liked him for more than just the sex and the corpse disposal, despite the fact that—at twenty-two—he was only half her age.

He put the phone back in his pocket. Then he got in his car and drove five miles from Hollywood to Studio City.

He parked in a residential neighborhood and got out. He had come here to take a walk. He walked to stay in shape. He had a gym membership, and he went to the gym for at least an hour every day, but he liked to walk for at least an hour outdoors every day, also.

He didn't see anyone else on foot, and traffic on the quiet streets was minimal.

He grabbed a maroon hooded jacket from the back of his car and put it on. He liked the jacket because it had several deep pockets. He liked the hood for the anonymity it provided. He liked the color maroon because he figured it didn't make him look sinister the way a black or even a gray hoodie would.

Octavio pulled the hood up over his head and took off walking. He retrieved a pair of gloves from one of his pockets and put them on.

Nearly every house he passed had a streetside mailbox in front of it. All of those mailboxes had numbers on them, and some of them also featured family names. If the name appeared to be Jewish (Cohen, Greenberg, Schwartz, etc.), he inserted into the mailbox one of the folded sheets of paper that he carried in one of his jacket's interior pockets. The sheets of paper were white. On each was a black swastika. Printed beneath the swastikas, in bold black letters, were the words ALL JEWS ARE VERMIN! DEATH TO ALL JEWISH RATS!

Octavio did not hate Jewish people any more than he hated other people. He hated all ethnic groups, races, and religions equally. In other neighborhoods, he distributed KILL WHITEY leaflets, CRUCIFY THE CHRISTIANS, and DEATH TO ALL DIRTY BLACKS.

Octavio whistled while he walked.

Occasionally dogs barked at him from porches, yards, and doghouses behind fences or walls. If this happened when no one was looking (which was almost always), he retrieved one of the many dog biscuits he carried in his pockets and tossed it to the dog.

Octavio liked dogs, but they were man's best friend, and in the interest of contributing to the downfall of society, the dog biscuits were laced with cyanide. All of the dogs would die a horrible death.

The deaths of so many pets would spread despair throughout the neighborhood—and possibly anger and paranoia would spread, too. Octavio hoped that those who did not own pets would be suspected of killing the dogs by those who did.

He had so much fun he lost track of time. When he finally checked his phone, he discovered that he had been walking for over two hours. The time was now 1:24 p.m. Verna had told him last night that she would be writing all day today and not to bother her until at least nine o'clock tonight.

He went to the gym. He had numerous e-books in the library on his phone. He spent two hours reading a Dean Koontz thriller while riding a stationary bike and walking on a treadmill. Octavio did not lift weights. He had no interest in bulking up. He only did cardio exercises to stay thin for his auditions.

By the time he got home, it was after four p.m. He didn't hear any noises coming from Verna's apartment upstairs. *Undoubtedly writing,* he thought. *Working on one of her screenplays.* He was looking forward to seeing her, but that was still about five hours away.

He took a nap. He woke up later and checked his phone: 6:18 p.m. He had slept for over two hours.

He brushed his teeth. He made a sandwich and ate it. He brushed his teeth again. Then he went back out to his car and drove around Hollywood for a while.

A sign in the yard of a two-story Spanish house caught his attention: LADY SERENITY'S BRIC-A-BRAC. Apparently it was a business that someone was operating from their home.

Only one vehicle was parked in the driveway: a dark-green SUV. Octavio parked behind the SUV and got out of his car.

The house had a tile roof and casement windows. Palm trees cast shadows against the stucco walls in the light of early evening.

Octavio went to the front entrance and rang the doorbell. He saw a sticker for a security-system company on the window by the door.

Moments later, a woman spoke to him through an intercom box. "The door's unlocked. Come on in."

Octavio stepped inside. Classical piano music was playing at low volume over a speaker system. He found himself surrounded by porcelain figurines, and felt as if he had somehow walked back through time into a bygone era. He saw painted miniatures and old photographs in frames, exquisitely decorated teacups and small vases, and artful arrangements of feathers and wax flowers under glass domes.

He began walking around, examining some of the merchandise displayed on tables, shelves, mantelpieces, and behind glass in curio cabinets. He saw an abundance of wondrous artifacts in various stages of preservation and disrepair: antique perfume bottles; first-edition books; old daggers with corroded blades; gramophones with tarnished horns; sparkling silverware; and much more.

He saw one item—an old typewriter—and immediately thought: *I bet Verna would love this.* He approached the old typewriter for a closer inspection. It was an Underwood No. 5, covered in dust and obviously neglected. In many places its black paint had been chipped away. None of its keys were missing, however. He wondered if the thing still even worked. He didn't see a price tag on it anywhere.

And then a stunningly beautiful woman entered the room. "Hi! I'm Serenity." She smiled. Her smile was dazzling. "Welcome to my store."

Serenity, maybe thirty, had long black hair and bright green eyes. Her face reminded him of mythological goddesses he had seen portrayed in classical art. She wore tight black jeans and a black T-shirt. Her body was lean, and he thought her breasts were perfect. He could see her nipples straining against her shirt.

"What's your name?"

"Octavio."

"See anything in here that interests you?"

"Yes. This old typewriter. Do you know if it works?"

Serenity shrugged. "I have no idea. I'm not even sure it's meant to work. It's an antique. At this point, maybe it's meant to be a display piece."

"A display piece?"

"Yes. But I'm sure it can be restored. Clean it up, replace a few parts, tighten some screws, and then you can write your great American novel. Are you a writer, Octavio?"

"No. I'm an actor. Well, an aspiring actor, anyway. Right now I work for a medical waste disposal company. My girlfriend's a writer. I want to buy the typewriter for my girlfriend."

Serenity smiled. "My husband was a writer."

"Was?"

"Yes. He died a few years back, not long after our daughter was born. Plane crash."

"I'm sorry to hear that."

"Thanks. It was tough, but Kaylie and I are getting by okay."

"How old is she?"

"Six. In first grade already. She has no memory of her father, but it had always been a dream of his to own an antique store. His life-insurance policy paid off the mortgage on this place, so now Kaylie and I live upstairs, and I run this antique store down here on the first floor."

A beautiful little girl entered the room. She had long black hair and bright green eyes. "Mommy, can we have pizza for dinner tonight?"

"Of course we can. And say hello to our new friend, Octavio."

The little girl looked up at him, and smiled. "Hello."

Octavio smiled back at her. "Hello. You must be Kaylie. It's great to meet you." Then he looked at her mother. "How much do you want for the typewriter?"

She told him a low price.

Octavio paid with cash. Then he carried the typewriter—a deceptively heavy machine—out to his car and left.

He arrived back home at 7:51 p.m. He still had over an hour to kill before he could go upstairs and see Verna.

He put the typewriter on his kitchen table. He cleaned it with a damp rag and some paper towels. It looked a little better without the dust on it, but not much. He decided to make the typewriter's restoration a future project. At some point in the future, he would strip it and clean its individual components with fine brushes and turpentine. He would either fix or replace any and all broken parts. He would sand away the old paint and use a spray gun to apply a new coat of black paint to its body. He wanted the typewriter to be fine enough for a museum whenever he finally gave it to Verna.

He brushed his teeth. He took his third shower of the day and shaved for the second time. He dressed in clean clothes.

He drank a beer and watched TV until fifteen after nine. Then he walked upstairs and knocked on Verna's apartment door.

She opened the door naked and covered in blood. She held a carving knife in one hand and a woman's severed head by the hair in the other. She smiled. "You're late."

Octavio smiled back. "I didn't want to seem too eager."

He looked down at the severed head she was holding. Blood still dripped from the neck stump onto the living room's hardwood floor. "I see you've been doing more than just working on your screenplay."

"I needed some inspiration," Verna said. "So I went out and found her in a bar. Also, I needed something to cook us for dinner tonight. Come on in."

Octavio stepped inside. "She smells delicious."

Verna closed the door and locked it.

***

On Sunday afternoon, Serenity took Kaylie out for lunch at a small diner called Lou's Cottage in Hollywood. Serenity ordered apple-baked ham and french fries. Kaylie ordered pancakes with a side dish of macaroni and cheese. While they were eating, Kaylie said, "Look, Mommy. There's Octavio."

Serenity turned her head in the direction that Kaylie was looking and saw the man to whom she had sold the old typewriter the day before. He was sitting at a table with a woman who appeared to be about twice his age. Neither was eating. Octavio was drinking a cup of coffee. The woman was typing furiously on a laptop. Octavio had told her that his girlfriend was a writer, but if this woman were his girlfriend, she did not look anything like what Serenity would have expected. The woman wasn't ugly, but she was very plain-looking and a far cry from beautiful, while Octavio, on the other hand, was half her age and as handsome as any actor vying for stardom in the City of Angels.

Kaylie and Serenity finished their food. As they were leaving, Octavio looked up at them and smiled. "Hi,

Kaylie," he said. "Hi, Serenity. This is my girlfriend, Verna—the writer I was telling you about."

"It's nice to meet you, Verna," Serenity said. "Are you working on a novel?"

Verna looked up briefly at them both. She didn't smile. Then she looked back down at her laptop. "No. A screenplay." She resumed typing.

"Are you open later today?" Octavio asked Serenity. "I'd like to bring Verna to your store and let her look around."

"No. We're closed on Sundays. But we'll be home in a little while. So if you want to stop by and look around the store, just ring the doorbell. I'll come down and let you in."

"That wouldn't be a problem?"

Serenity shook her head. "Not at all."

Octavio sipped his coffee. "It might be later this evening, though. Is that okay?"

"How late are you talking?"

"Probably about eight or nine o'clock tonight."

Serenity smiled. "Sure, that's okay. We stay up late."

Octavio smiled back. "Great! We'll see you tonight."

Kaylie and Serenity left. They went to an ice-cream parlor for dessert.

***

Kaylie was downstairs helping her mother with the dusting of the antique store when the doorbell rang. She was nowhere close to sleepy yet, but she could see beyond the windows that night had fallen.

Serenity checked her phone. The time was 8:54 p.m. "That must be Octavio and Verna." She went to the front door and opened it.

A light rain was falling and both of them had hoods over their heads. Octavio wore the maroon hoodie she had seen him wearing yesterday; Verna's hoodie was black.

Serenity smiled. "Hi! Come on in."

Octavio turned to Verna. "After you."

She entered the store. He followed her inside.

Serenity closed the door behind them. "Kaylie and I were just dusting. Feel free to look around the store. If you need any help with anything, just let me—"

Octavio clubbed her alongside the head with a silencer-fitted pistol and she dropped to the floor, unconscious.

"Put her in the car," Verna said. "I'll go get the girl."

***

"Mommy?" *Kaylie's voice.*

Serenity opened her eyes. She had a violent headache and saw the silhouette of her daughter sitting across from her in a darkened room. The last thing she remembered was Octavio raising a pistol and swinging it at her head, then blackness.

"Mommy? Are you awake yet?"

"Yes, Kaylie. I'm awake. Where are we?"

"We're in a bathroom. The bad people tied us up in a bathroom and turned out the light."

Serenity was sitting on a chair. She tried to get up, but could not. She realized she was not merely sitting on the chair; she was tied to it. Ropes bound her chest and waist, and more ropes were tied across her thighs, securing her to the seat. Her arms were fastened to the arms of the chair below her elbows and again at her wrists.

"Are you okay, Kaylie? Did they hurt you?"

"I'm scared, Mommy. I wanna go home."

Serenity heard the door open behind her. Someone turned on the light. She and her daughter were tied to chairs beside an old clawfoot bathtub.

Then Verna and Octavio entered her field of vision. Verna was totally naked except for a pair of yellow rain boots. She held a carving knife in one hand and a straight razor in the other. Octavio, fully dressed, was holding his silencer-fitted pistol and a roll of duct tape.

"Which one do you want?" Verna asked Octavio.

"The little girl," he said. "I want Kaylie."

"There's a twin bed up in the attic," Verna said.

"That's okay," he said. "I have a twin bed downstairs in my apartment."

She cocked her head. "You do?"

"Yes. Spare bedroom."

"Ah, okay. I didn't know that."

"Listen!" Serenity said. "I have some money. Quite a bit of money. So if you'll just let us go, I'll pay you a lot of money, and I promise that I won't say anything about any of this to anybody."

Verna looked at Octavio. "Tape her fucking mouth shut."

Octavio did. Then he dragged Kaylie out of the bathroom by her chair and closed the door.

Verna, standing in front of Serenity, set the carving knife on the sink and raised the straight razor. "Ready to have some fun?"

Serenity started crying and closed her eyes, but Verna forced them open.

***

Several hours later, after torturing, killing, and dismembering Serenity in the clawfoot tub, Verna took a shower in the other bathroom. Then she got dressed and went down the staircase that was probably once the centerpiece of the old house but was now only a path from her apartment to Octavio's.

His door was locked, but she had a key. She let herself in.

His apartment, as always, was clean but smelled like a slaughterhouse. She saw a beautiful old typewriter sitting on the kitchen table.

She had never been in the spare bedroom he mentioned earlier, but she knew where it was. She went to the closed door of the spare bedroom. It wasn't locked. She opened the door and stepped into the room.

Verna was glad she had put her rain boots back on. There was so much blood on the walls, floor, and ceiling that the room looked like someone had splashed red paint all over the place. There were bones scattered everywhere. There were pieces of organs stuck to the bloody walls. There were even chunks of flesh hanging like red stalactites from the ceiling.

Octavio, covered in blood, lay naked atop the blood-soaked twin bed, holding Kaylie's severed head on his chest. The only other parts of her body still recognizable as human remains were the two hands still roped to the bedposts.

"Oh my god," Verna said. "That old typewriter on your kitchen table is amazing."

Octavio set Kaylie's head aside. "I'm glad you like it. I bought it just for you. I'm going to restore it first, though, before I give it to you."

"Thank you so much," Verna said. "Are you hungry?"

"Yes. Famished, actually."

"Good. Dinner will be ready in about an hour. I hope you like antiques dealers."

Octavio smiled. "That sounds delicious."

## About the Author

Brian Bowyer has been writing stories and music for most of his life. He has lived throughout the United States. He has worked as a janitor, a banker, a bartender, a bouncer, and a bomb maker for a coal-testing laboratory. He currently lives and writes in Ohio. You can contact him at brian.bowyer@hotmail.com.

Printed in Great Britain
by Amazon